Toby Travis Scores

P W Wolfendale

Published by Sante Books, 2023.

This is a work of fiction. Similarities to real people, places, or events are entirely coincidental.

TOBY TRAVIS SCORES

First edition. May 27, 2023.

ISBN: 979-8223601463

Written by P W Wolfendale.

Acknowledgement

Christopher Bedson...William McMullan...Benjamin McMullan

I would like to thank my three grandchildren at present, Christopher, William and Benjamin, for giving me the inspiration needed to write this book. I have used their names in the book to remind me of the love their step-grandmother and I share with them.

In years to come when I have passed over to the other side, I would like to think that occasionally they will be reminded of their grandad by reading a few chapters from my book. We all go back many generations, so what better way than being able to remind ourselves of this fact by putting pen to paper?

I believe we have all got a book or two within our capability; it is just a case of finding the time in our busy schedules. All these pull-up a sandbag stories are hidden away somewhere at the back of our minds.

CHAPTER 1

TOBY MEETS MARY

It was 6.30 am and 13-year-old Toby was out of bed sharply to the sound of his alarm clock, and then within the blink of an eye, raced down the road on his bicycle to do his paper round on a beautiful summer's day. "Morning Toby," could be heard from one of the neighbours that was walking peacefully with her dog, and at the same time, getting some good old British fresh air into her lungs. "Morning Mrs Green," replied Toby, purely out of politeness as was the way Toby had been brought up by his mother; always be polite was Toby's philosophy.

Toby lived with his 41-year-old mother and his 15-year-old sister in a semi-detached house on a middle-class housing estate; 45 Primrose Avenue to be more precise in a small town called Yelling. Unfortunately for Toby and his sister, his father passed away just months before Toby was born due to a long-term incurable illness. It is now 6.45 am and Toby could be seen propping his bike up against the wall of the Paper shop. Without much thought and not a care in the world, Toby clatterers his way through the front door to the sound of the bell that would warn the shopkeeper that they had a customer.

"Oh, it's you, Toby," said the shopkeeper sounding tremendously disappointed that it wasn't a paying customer. "Get yourself in the back Toby, your papers and magazines are waiting for you; they're all in order so don't mix them up."

"Ok Mrs Callaghan," said Toby gratefully. Mrs Callaghan was Toby's neighbour from No 47 who also had a beautiful 15-year-old daughter named Mary, someone that Toby had a bit of a shine for. With his sturdy yellow bag that was full to the brim with yesterday's news, Toby made his way out of the shop. "Bye Mrs Callaghan," said Toby.

"Bye Toby, be careful on those busy roads, see you tomorrow." It took Toby about 45 minutes to complete his paper round. The route would be mapped-out carefully so that Toby would finish his paper round on Primrose Avenue the place where he lived. Outside Toby's house, and with the time now 7.30 am, the avenue was coming alive. Toby got a glimpse of the curtain twitchers at No 43, the home of two elderly people called Bob and Brenda

Wilkinson; even at the sound of the drop of a hat falling to the floor, Bob and Brenda would always be peeping around the corner of the curtains. They were two warm loving people with time on their hands, people that Toby would run an errand for in their time of need. Toby would always make a special effort to glance up at the bedroom window of No 47, hoping to get a glimpse of Mary getting ready for school; not that he was a pervert or anything like that. On this occasion, Toby was in luck. With a huge smile and raised eyebrows Mary waved excitedly at Toby. This is one of the first times that Toby felt out of his comfort zone; this unexpected warm welcome from Mary had Toby blushing. Toby sat motionless on his bicycle for what seemed an eternity with his eyes fixed on Mary's bedroom window. Unfortunately, Toby's lack of confidence was now getting the better of him so much that he was getting himself into a right pickle; as soon as he went to push his bike over the edge of the kerb, he fell embarrassingly onto his drive scuffing his hands to protect his fall; not sure what hurt the most, his hands or his pride. A look of concern from Mary with a slight chuckle under her breath was something that Toby would have to live with.

Toby made his way into his house to be welcomed by his mum cooking breakfast for Toby and his sister Holly. Without Toby knowing, Holly was looking through the front room window at the same time that Toby fell off his bike but felt bringing up the subject would have caused Toby more embarrassment. "Get sat down Toby," said his mum, "I've made you sausage, egg and bacon."

"Thanks, Mum," said Toby still feeling sheepish.

"What's up with you this morning Toby," said Holly inquisitively.

"Nothing at all just tumbled off my bike on the drive."

"Are you ok?" asked his mum handing Toby his breakfast with a look of concern on her face.

"Yes, just a few scratches on my hands, I'll live, but probably not recommended."

Toby's mum made her way out of the kitchen area to get her belongings together before going to her part-time job at the local Laundrette In the town. This now gave Holly the ideal opportunity to continue with her quizzing. "Call it women's intuition if you like Toby, but I can tell there is something on your mind. So come on, tell me what's really on your mind. You were looking like you had the weight of the world on your shoulders when you came through the door.

"There's nothing wrong, nothing at all," said Toby feeling uncomfortable with Mary's questions.

"I saw you fall off your bike Toby, I was looking through the front room window, I saw you looking up at Mary's bedroom window, there was definitely some biology going on there."

"Biology, what do you mean biology going on?"

"Don't worry yourself about it, Toby, just let's say, I saw a connection between you and Mary."

Toby was now feeling uneasy, and even more uncomfortable that Holly had seen him fall off his bike. "I just sort of froze for a minute Holly," said Toby being careful with his words. "It was like I was hypnotized, my legs turned to jelly, and then... well you saw what happened."

"Toby, you're falling in love," said Holly with a look that said it was quite normal. "Outside in the big wide world, there is always someone out there for each and every one of us; you've just got to look in the right places, and I don't mean sleazy bars. Fortunately for you Toby, you have just happened to have found your love right on your own doorstep."

"In love!" said Toby quietly, just in case their mum overheard their conversation.

"Yes Toby, in love, just get on with it, you're almost 14, it's called growing a pair, and please don't ask me what that means; you can work that one out for yourself."

"I've gone right off my breakfast now Holly; I don't think I could stomach it."

"Quiet, mum's coming back, I will talk to you more tonight in my room."

"Ok, I'd like that," said Toby staring at Holly.

"I'm off to work now you pair," don't forget to lock up, and get that breakfast eaten Toby, anybody would think you're in love." Toby and Holly just looked at each other trying to hold back their laughter until their mum had closed the front door.

At the Laundrette, Toby's mum Rose was still pondering over Toby's slightly bizarre behaviour at the breakfast table. "Morning Rose," was the cry that could just about be heard over the powering washing machines and dryers.

"Morning Hilda, Morning Marge," shouted Rose.

"How's things with you Rose?" said Marge looking for some gossip. Before long Marge and Hilda had the full attention of Rose with the launderette now managing itself. Anyone that knows Hilda and Marge would know they are the sort of people that would find fault with perfection. Aside from that, you would take anything they said with a pinch of salt.

Rose, Marge and Hilda, all sat down within inches of each other clutching their mugs of tea. Rose was the first to tell her story about Toby's strange behaviour. "He's in love," said Marge, you mark my word Rose; any man that's off his food is either in love... or up to no good. I remember my Harry coming home one day; he had been off his food for weeks, only seeing another woman at work so he was."

"Really!" said Rose feeling shocked, so what happened?"

"Well after doing some investigating, I managed to find out where she lived. While he was at work and without telling my husband, I packed his bags for him and took them around to her house. The look on her face was an absolute picture, Rose. I just threw all of his belongings that he possessed on her front doorstep, and that was the last I saw of him; she was welcome to him."

"What did she say?"

"She didn't, she didn't dare, I would have ripped her eyes out."

"Good for you," said Marge.

Rose who was a more refined lady was now feeling this conversation was not really appropriate for her to listen to anymore, so decided to change the subject to something more light-hearted, like the price of a loaf of bread these days.

Mean while at the Lakeside County Secondary School, Toby was getting changed for PT in the changing rooms with all of his classmates; about 30 in all. "Ok you lot, get yourselves in the gym now," yelled Mr Symonds. "Come on, get a move on, and that includes you Travis, do I have to give you your own personal invitation?"

"No sir."

"Then get a move on now." In the meantime at Lilly Pink Secondary School for girls, sat at her desk, Mary was chatting away to her best friend Lucy; trying not to be compromised by the ever-eagled-eyed school teacher. Mary and Lucy tried to keep their conversation to a whisper. "I think I have a secret admirer," said Mary with a sort of naughty childish look on her face.

"Wow! Really," said Lucy now giving Mary her full attention. "Is it someone I know?"

"I don't think so; he goes to the Lakeside Secondary School for boys, the one about a mile from here."

"What's his name then?" asked Lucy feeling intrigued at Mary's news. "Go on them Mary, tell me, the suspense is killing me."

"Ok then Lucy, hold your horses. His name is Toby, Toby Travis, my next-door neighbour. He's really good looking: about medium height, dark short hair, and slim build, green eyes and walks with a limp."

"A limp!" said Lucy rolling back her eyes.

"Only joking, he hasn't really got a limp."

"Does he have big feet, Mary?"

"Yes, and I know where you're going with this question Lucy, let's not go down that road."

"Ooh, touched a raw nerve have I?" replied Lucy chuckling out loud. Just then Mrs Douglas the teacher caught sight of Lucy's unacceptable behaviour. "What on earth are you chuckling at Lucy," said Mrs Douglas angrily.

"Sorry miss, just something my mum said this morning."

"Then keep your thoughts to yourself, and keep your noise down."

"Go on then Mary, carry on," said Lucy.

"Well, I saw him looking up at my bedroom window this morning after his paper round,"

"So he's a pervert then, my god Mary, you can't half pick 'em."

"Oh Lucy, don't be so dense, Toby is a quiet lad, the sort of lad that butter wouldn't melt in his mouth, I just feel he has taken a bit of a shine to me, I could be imagining it though, I hope I'm not."

"So what did you do when the pervert, sorry I meant Toby looked up at your bedroom window?"

"Will you stop calling him a pervert Lucy before we fall out big time. I just waved and smiled at him like I was enjoying his attention."

"And were you enjoying his attention, Mary?"

"Well of course I was, wouldn't you? I won't lie to you Lucy, it felt really good, it made me feel important... I felt like a million dollars...I felt like I wanted to hold his hand and wander off into our own little world, just having a chat about anything or nothing. It was a feeling that I have never felt before," described Mary.

"You're in Love Mary, one hundred percent in love."

"Pardon me," said Mary at Lucy's remark. "How would I know; I've never been in love before. I'm only 15 years old Lucy; is it normal to fall in love at such a young age?"

"If you have never felt this way before then yes, why not, I'm sure you can fall in love at any age Mary, it might be puppy love, or..."

"Or what?" Asked Mary starting to feel worried about what Lucy was going to say next.

"Or, or the real thing, Mary."

Meanwhile, back at the Lakeside Secondary School, the PT teacher Mr Symonds had an announcement to make at the end of the PT session. With everyone now getting changed back into their school uniforms, Mr Symonds shouted from the door of the changing room.

"I'm not sure how many of you know, but the school football team is doing extremely well at the moment. We are second in the league table with one game to go, but most of all, we are in the semi-final of the four counties cup. We have never won this cup before, but feel this is our best chance ever to win some silver wear. We already have a well-established team but feel there is still room for more quality, a quality that I believe is out there somewhere. For anyone who thinks they have what it takes to get a place in the school football team, there will be trials after school at 3.30 pm. If you have your boots with you then bring them, if not, then any suitable footwear will be ok."

"What about it, Toby?" asked Liam Fenwick, one of Toby's best friends.

"Not sure if I'm good enough for the team Liam, anyway I haven't got a pair of football boots and my mum can't really afford to buy me any," said Toby pitifully, but he understood his mother's position.

"Well, you've got nothing to lose if you don't make it Toby, better to have tried and failed than not tried at all is a famous saying I have heard somewhere or other."

"You are so correct Liam," said Toby with a huge smile of determination on his face. "I can play in my school shoes." It was now 3 pm and both the girl's and boys' school were now at the end of their school day. Toby was off to the school football trials and Mary was walking home with her best friend Lucy. With Mary's mum still working until 5 pm, Mary decided to pop into Archie's Confectioneries where her mum worked and Toby did his paper round. "Why don't you ask your mum if it would be ok to invite Toby round for tea," said Lucy mischievously.

"Stop it, Lucy," said Mary with her mouth now open wide with shock. "It's not going to happen so let's leave it at that."

"Oh, come on Mary, what have you to lose, better to have tried and failed than not tried at all."

"Now where have I heard that saying before Lucy?"

"I've no idea Mary, but it's true."

"I just felt I heard someone say it this afternoon, never mind, just forget it, I must be going mad." Mary and Lucy entered the corner shop. "Hi Darling, hi Lucy," said Mary's mum happy to see her daughter.

"Hi Mrs Callaghan," said Lucy. "Mary has something she would like to ask you."

"Lucy!" said Mary with a disgusted look on her face.

"What is it?" said Mary's mum inquisitively.

"Oh it's nothing Mum; it's just Lucy being silly."

"Now don't give me that Mary, if you can't talk to your mum, then who can you talk to Mary?" In the meantime Lucy was acting all coy and innocent, standing well away from the action that was about to take place. "Ok, Ok," said Mary reluctantly. "I was wondering if at some time, and whenever it is possible, and I don't mind if you say no."

"What is it, Mary? I'm feeling worried now about what you are going to ask me."

"Well, you know Toby from No 45 next door to us."

"Yes, of course I do, and a lovely lad at that may I add."

"Well.... I was wondering if I could invite him around for tea one evening."

"Yes, of course," said Mary's mum now feeling relieved. "When did he say he would like to come around?"

"He doesn't know yet."

"What do you mean he doesn't know yet, do you mean he doesn't know when he will be available, is that what you mean?"

"No, it means I haven't asked him yet."

"Then how do you know he's in favour of coming around for tea if you haven't asked him?"

"I don't know Mum, but I guess I will never know unless I invite him."

"This whole thing seems half-baked to me Mary. I'll tell you what; Toby normally pops into the shop on his way home from school, to buy some sweets. If I see him, I will ask him if he would like to join us for tea."

"Aww thanks' mum, that would be nice; one thing though."

"And what's that Mary?"

"Could you make sure that it sounds like it's your idea Mum and not mine?"

"Yes, of course, discretion is something I am good at Mary, catch you later."

"Bye Mrs Callaghan," said Lucy feeling proud that her cunning plan had worked.

Back at Lakeside Secondary School, the football trials were about to begin. Mr Symonds and Mr Mann were the two teachers in charge of getting Lakeside to the top of the league, and winning the four counties cup... a task that has never been achieved before in their history. The warm-up was in full force with about 20 or more hopefuls trying to make the school football team, along with the already reputable well-established players. "Ok listen up," said Mr Symonds, "you'll be split into 2 teams of 11 players and then I will swap you around at my discretion: I'm looking for your ability to pass the ball, run with the ball, pick out a pass, speed and determination, and eye for goal, being able to read and control the game; tough tackling is also a good contribution but without breaking someone's leg, are there any questions? No, then get yourself on to the field"

"Are you ready Toby?" said Liam the football team captain.

"Ready as I will ever be Liam; let's get this show on the road." To be brutally honest, Toby looked like he had just come in from a night out on the town: grey school trousers, school shoes and a green school football shirt. A watchful eye from the two school teachers that were making notes could be seen from afar.

"Liam Fenwick, looking good as usual," said Nick Symonds.

"Yes, I have to agree," replied Andrew Mann, 'speed to burn that one, and a great level of skill."

"I also like the look of Mat White, strong in the air, would make a terrific Centre Back, could be good for competition in that position."

"What do you think of Gus Breeze?" asked Andrew.

"He holds the ball well; I believe he would be good in the midfield area."

"Travis, get yourself on the pitch lad, Gus, you can come off now, I think you've made a case for the midfield position," said Mr Symonds. It was now time for Toby to show his football skills that he had doubts about. Within minutes it wasn't looking good for Toby as his doubts were confirmed; playing in his school shoes, and no matter where he played or what he did, he struggled to make an impression on Mr Symonds and Mr Mann. "Well at least we can count Toby Travis out, maybe he would be better at Netball," said Nick laughing to anyone that could hear him.

"Yes, have to agree with you Nick, no talent at all that one." If only Toby could hear them, maybe one day those cruel remarks would come back to haunt them. It was now time to get changed and head home before finding out tomorrow if Toby had made the football team. Toby caught up with Liam momentarily. "What do you think Toby?" asked Liam.

"Not sure, I gave it my best, will have to wait and see, I'm not holding out much hope though, I wish I possessed your skills, Liam, I can definitely see why you have been appointed Captain of the team."

"Thanks for that Toby, means a lot, anyway I will catch you tomorrow."

"See you Liam; I'll keep my fingers crossed." Meanwhile, Mary was now at home in her bedroom on her laptop doing her homework, and in a nice way, trying to forget about Toby; what she was really doing was clock watching, knowing that her mum would be home soon with some sort of news.

It was close to 5 pm, the time Mary's mum, Jill would be leaving the shop and making her way home. All of a sudden, the shop door opened with the familiar sound of the bell once more. "Hi Mrs Callaghan," said Toby, "just dropped- in to buy some sweets."

"Running late today are we Toby?" said Jill.

"Yes, I've been having football trials, I am hoping to make the school football team, I should find out tomorrow."

"Oh well, I wish you luck with that Toby, getting on to another subject. What will you be having for tea tonight Toby?"

"Not sure, nothing special, not that I don't eat well, my mum sometimes waits until I get home and then asks me what I would like, why do you ask?"

"Oh, sorry if I sounded nosey Toby, it wasn't meant to sound like that, I'm pretty sure you do eat well. I was just wondering, how would you like to join my family and me tonight, we are having Pizza, I'm sure Mary would enjoy your company, In fact, now I come to think about it, I will not take no as an answer; pop around about 6.30 tonight, I will look forward to seeing you then." Toby never even had time to draw breath before his mind was made up for him.

"Ok Mrs Callaghan," said Toby now feeling ultra nervous, "I will see you this evening, look forward to it."

Mary was still clock-watching when suddenly, she heard her mum's car turning into their driveway. This was the moment Mary had been waiting for over the last two hours. Within seconds, Mary heard the front door open. "Hi Mary, you ok?" shouted her mum from the foot of the stairs.

"Yes, just doing some homework mum, be down in a second." Mary was actually on her mobile phone, keeping Lucy informed. "I must go now Lucy, mums back, I will call you later."

"Ok Mary, let me know what happens," said Lucy excitingly.

"Catch you later Holly, bye, for now, love you." To Mary, it didn't sound like there wasn't anything important that her mum had to say otherwise she would have said so right away, however, her mum was being very discreet; knowing that her daughter was keen to find out if she had spoken to Toby, meant she wasn't in a rush to tell Mary. Minutes later Mary made her way down the stairs into the dining area where her mum was preparing tea. "Hi mum," said Mary with a cuddle. "How are things? Had a good day mum?"

"Yes Mary, I only spoke to you about an hour ago, what's with all the questions?"

"Nothing, I was Just wondering; no reason behind my reasoning Mum."

"Anyway, would you mind setting the table Mary, your father will be home soon."

"Will do, I'll do it right away."

"Oh Mary, I almost forgot, could you set one extra place please, we have one additional mouth to feed tonight; Toby from No 45 said he will love to join us."

"What! Please say you're joking Mum."

"No, I'm not joking Mary; he will be here in about an hour, don't look so horrified."

"Horrified Mum, horrified? I do not believe you sometimes, I meant maybe next week or something like that; not tonight: I need to get showered, make-up, clean clothes, and wash my hair; it's just not going to happen in an hour.

Mary started to utter under her breath. *"Ok calm down Mary, this is just my worst nightmare, I will wake up in a minute and everything will be fine.* Ok, I'm off upstairs to sort myself out now mum, I will do my best not to get all flustered."

Back at Toby's house, it was much the same. "Mum, have you got a moment, I've been invited to Mary's house next door for tea."

"What's all that about then, that's a first?"

"Not sure, and excuse me for sounding a little dismissive, but for some unknown reason and right out of the blue, Mrs Callaghan asked me if I fancied coming round for tea. It was when I called at the shop on my way home from school; I didn't even seem to have any choice in the matter; before I could say anything, I heard, great see you at 6.30."

"Oh well Toby, one less mouth to feed."

"Where's Holly, mum?"

"Think she's upstairs in her bedroom."

"Cheers, mum." Before Toby's mum could say any more, Toby was upstairs quicker than a rat up a drain pipe. "Hi Toby," said Holly as Toby entered her room, "everything ok?"

"Well sort of. The thing is, well let's just say, erm, I haven't got as much time to chat with you as we suggested this morning."

"Why's that then Toby what could have possibly changed since I spoke to you this morning."

"Well for some unknown reason I've been invited to have tea with Mary tonight, and I haven't got a clue why or enough time to explain the day I have had, all I know is that I need to be there for about 6.30."

"Wow! You don't waste much time do you, Toby."

"It's not like that Holly; I've got no idea why Mrs Callaghan invited me round for tea. Before I could even say I will need to think about it, she said, well that's it, settled then, will see you at 6.30. I will explain it all later Holly, must dash now, I need to get ready." 6.30 arrived in quick time. Toby took the long journey of about 5 metres to Mary's house. Ding Dong went the bell that was clearly heard by Mary in her bedroom, was just putting the finishing touches to her make-up. The front door opened only for Toby to be greeted by Mary's father Brian. "Hello, it must be Toby, am I correct?"

"Yes," answered Toby feeling ill at ease.

"Well, my name is Brian, Mary's father, please step inside and take a seat in the living room, Toby."

"Mary, Toby's here," shouted her father. Toby sat on the two-seated sofa as instructed and waited for Mary to show her face.

"Ok, just give me a couple minutes Dad; tell Toby I will be with him shortly."This was the first time that Toby was now starting to question the motive of why he was invited, it was all starting to fall into place now; it was to be their first date with a little help from Mary's mum.... and of course Lucy.

Within minutes, Mary arrived in the living room feeling as anxious as Toby, and at the same time, not really knowing where to sit. However, that problem was soon to be resolved as Mary's mum once more took the only available seat apart from the seat next to Toby. I'm sure Toby wasn't going to complain when Mary took the seat next to him. You could feel the nervy tension between Mary and Toby as they were only inches apart. Although Toby and Mary had been friends for some years, it was only now that their hormones were kicking in. "Shall we make our way into the dining room?" said Mrs Callaghan in a kind of posh accent. Again, the seating options were limited; where does one sit at the dining table, leave it to Mum, she will sort it out. "Brian you can sit at the head of the table and I will sit at the other end, Mary and Toby, you can sit opposite each other. Toby just waited for a second until everyone else was seated. "Well are you going to sit down or just stand there hovering?" asked Brian firmly."

"Dad," said Mary, "don't be so rude."

"I wasn't being rude Mary, just making a very valid point."

"No, I hadn't planned on standing up all night Mr Callaghan; I just thought it would be better to wait until everyone else had taken their seat."

"Very polite of you Toby," said Mary's mum, "Nice to see good manners."

"My God Jill, you don't need to go over the top," said Brian, "let the lad feel at home instead of going on about his good manners."

"I am not going over the top Brian; it is nice to see good manners. It was your rudeness that sparked it all off.

"Well now I would like to end it, so let's hear no more about it, please." Toby and Mary just looked at each other like World War Three was about to take place. "Would you like a drink with your Pizza, Toby?" asked Mrs Callaghan.

"Yes, that would be nice thank you, Coca Cola please."

"Same for me Mum," said Mary taking advantage of her mum's hospitality.

Toby and Mary were very careful in what they said; it was such an awkward situation. "So Toby, what was your day like?" asked Mr Callaghan drumming up a conversation. Toby explained his football trials that had Mr Callaghan transfixed as he too liked football. "So, what position do you play Toby?"

"Normally anywhere up front: centre forward, right wing, they are my preferred positions."

"Well let's hope you make the team Toby; I wish you good luck."

"Thank you Mr Callaghan."

The table was now feeling empty and apart from Toby dropping a piece of Pizza on the floor, all went well. "Would it be ok for Toby to come up to my bedroom mum?" asked Mary.

"Yes of course, but let's say half an hour and no more; then I think it would be time for Toby to go home. You ok with that Brian?"

"Yes, very fair Jill, nice to see we are finally agreeing on something."

"Yes, it makes a nice change Brian," said Jill rolling her eyes and still trying to have the last word on the subject. "Anyway Mary, are you ok with that?"

"Yes, thanks, Mum." This was an opportunity for Toby and Mary to chat about their feelings for each other, to find out their interests, their likes and dislikes. Mary sat down on the edge of her soft comfy bed still feeling slightly insecure "Would you like to join me, Toby, we can go onto my laptop and check things out."

"That would be nice," replied Toby feeling a little more relaxed. Toby should have now been sitting inches away from Mary but unfortunately, because Toby jumped on the bed with the force of an Elephant, Mary was now catapulted onto the floor. "Oh my God, I am so sorry Mary, are you ok?"

"Just a flesh wound Toby, I'm sure I will live," said Mary rubbing her head. Toby assisted Mary in helping her back onto the bed and continued with his apologies. With no mummy and daddy looking on, Toby and Mary were undoubtedly feeling more confident with each other. "So how old are you Mary?"

"I was 15 last month."

"Oh, I see, well happy birthday for last month Mary."

"Thank you, Toby, and how old are you?"

"Well, if I manage to live for another two weeks, I will be 14."

"Toby you daft thing, don't talk like that. Anyway, that's great news; I can feel a birthday present coming on."

"Are you ok with the age gap Mary?"

"Yes, as long as you are. There is just over 1 year between us and I don't mind being older than you; you hear about it all the time, if fact, my mum is 2 years older than my dad."

"I'm glad about that; I've got no problem with it either."

At this point, and maybe by chance, they got even closer to each other as they both had their heads in the laptop. Within seconds of their eyes beadily meeting; a small but passionate kiss was planted on their lips. "Does this mean we're now officially dating Mary?"

"Yes, I guess so, well that's if you want to Toby,"

"Yes, I would like that Mary; I would like that very much." Before you knew it, their time together had ebbed away. "Toby, are you ready, time to go home love," shouted Mary's mum. Deep down inside, Mrs Callaghan knew that this would be the first of many dates between Toby and Mary, and hopefully a long-lasting relationship. As Toby came down the stairs with Mary close behind, you could feel the warmth of their relationship already developing; a smile of contentment on the face of Mrs Callaghan was a sign of her approval. After Toby had left, Mary couldn't wait a moment longer to call her best friend Lucy and tell her all the gossip. "Hi Lucy," said Mary ecstatically.

"How was it, Mary? And don't you dare miss anything out; I want to know every little bit of detail."

"Well, it was so uncomfortable at first Lucy, particularly with my mum and dad looking on at the dining table."

"And then what happened; were you playing footsie under the table, Mary?"

"Lucy! Behave yourself, will you. Well after our evening meal, my mum allowed us to go up to my bedroom for half an hour, so we could be alone."

"You're kidding me, Mary, this is better than watching a Romcom movie, I've never been so excited."

"Initially I sat on the edge of my bed and then invited Toby to join me, unfortunately, Toby sort of jumped onto the bed and then I fell off." Lucy could be heard on the other end of the phone laughing for Britain. "I'm so sorry for laughing Mary, but the way you described it was amazing, you should think of being a comedian, I am bent over with laughter."

"Well I suppose it was funny looking back on it now, but my head still feels sore Lucy."

"Well go on then Mary, this is a brilliant story, can't wait to hear the rest."

"Well Toby helped me to my feet and then we finally sat on the edge of the bed with my laptop before our heads were only inches apart."

"Oh my days, I'm lying on my bed now kicking my legs in the air, I can't believe what you are telling me."

"Well if you give me a second to finish what I was about to say, Lucy, I will tell you that we shared a passionate kiss on the lips, it was incredible! Toby is going to walk with me tomorrow morning as far as the bus stop on the way to school."

"You little Tiger Mary; so made up for you." Mary and Lucy chatted away for at least an hour before ending the call and getting some beauty sleep.

Back at Toby's house, Toby went straight to his sister's bedroom to tell her all about his night at the Callaghan's. It was meant to be a 'Birds and Bees' chat on how to build up your confidence before your first date; but unfortunately, because everything happened so quickly, Toby missed out a few chapters and went straight to chapter 20 of what to do on your first date. "I don't believe you sometimes Toby."

"What do you mean Holly?"

"Well I think the chat that I had prepared for you. may as well be thrown out of the window, seems like you don't need it."

"Sorry about that Holly, I had absolutely no idea what tonight was going to bring."

"No need to be sorry Toby, just glad it went well for you, but if you do need me for anything Toby, I'll be here for you; always willing to give good advice to my little brother."

"Less of the little, Holly, but thank you anyway."

The next morning at breakfast, Toby's mum was asking, "Toby, if you want a lift today, I can oblige, I am going to the Laundrette a little later today, if you get a move on I can give you a lift to school, and you Holly if you are ready; I can drop you off and then do a bit of shopping, save me doing an extra journey into the town later."

Holly was more than grateful for a lift, it would save her catching the bus some half a mile away, however, Toby had different ideas. Without indulging too much information about his night at the Callaghan's, he answered. "I'll be fine thanks mum, need to keep my fitness levels up for the school football team."

"Oh, ok Toby," said his mum thinking, *well done Toby, a good healthy decision.* "Oh my word, I had forgotten about the football trials, when will you find out if you have been selected?"

"We were told it would be sometime later-on today Mum." As Toby's mum was just about to leave, the doorbell rang. "Who can that be this time in the morning?" she said with a surprising look on her face. On opening the door, she was startled to see Mary standing on her doorstep with a beaming smile all ready for school. "Morning Mrs Travis," said Mary confidently. "Is Toby ready?"

"Ready!" ready for what may I ask?"

"Yes of course you may ask. Toby said he will walk with me to the school bus stop."

"What about your bike Toby, what are you doing with that?"

"I will push it Mum, and then when I get to Mary's bus stop, I will ride the rest of the journey to school."

"Oh I see," said Toby's mum smirking at her daughter Holly.

"Come on mum," said Holly, "let's get going."

"Don't forget to lock up Toby, best of luck with the football trials, see you later."

"Bye Mum."

"Bye Mrs Travis," said Mary politely. It was a short walk of about half a mile, the same bus stop that Holly would use as they were both at the same school. Holly was in the year above Mary, so would only get to see her at certain break times. Mary and Toby chit-chatted away about various likes and dislikes. Mary wasn't a keen football fan but was surprised how interesting she found the sport after Toby had explained it to her; she was being very supportive of Toby's quest to make the school football team. Mary found out more about Toby's dad and felt his pain that he has lived with all his life. As for Mary, well she has been lucky on the family side. Her father and mother are both caring parents with her father working as an accountant, and as we know, her mother works at the corner shop, probably just to get out of the house and earn some pocket money.

At the school bus stop, the chatting became more about school and not about their personal life. "Here's the bus now Mary."

"Oh Yeah, I think the overall size of it is a bit of a giveaway, Toby, what do you think?"

"Ok Mary, you don't need to be sarcastic, it doesn't suit you.

"I just couldn't let an opportunity like that go by without saying something Toby."

"Anyway, I will see you later Mary." Toby was still unsure whether or not to give Mary a Kiss in front of all her school friends and possibly compromise their relationship. Toby had nothing to worry about, within two shakes of a Lamb's tail, Mary kissed Toby on the side of his face with a kind of relief written on Toby's face; the decision to kiss Mary was now taken out of his hands.

"Wooooo!" could be heard from Mary's friends as she hopped onto the bus to a rapturous applause.

Back at the Launderette, Rose (Toby's Mum) was set upon by Hilda and Marge. "How's Toby, did you find out whether it was a girl that was causing him to lose his appetite Rose?" said Hilda as she launched into Rose. Kettle on, a brew made, they sat themselves down for the goss. "I think he is seeing the girl next door, Mary is her name," said Rose quietly. "He was invited to her house last night for tea by Mary's mum, and then this morning, well, he refused a lift to school so that he could walk Mary to the school bus stop."

"Oh Mary, what a beautiful name," said Marge.

"It's definitely puppy love Rose," said Hilda in a common type of tone, "you mark my word; before you know it, she will be baring a child."

"Mother Teresa!" said Rose panicking, "surely not."

"Do they teach sex education at the high schools today," said Marge adding more fuel to the fire.

"And how am I suppose to know that Marge?"

"Ask him when he comes home from school tonight; just sort of, well you know, bring up the subject, discreetly of course."

"Discreetly, you can't even spell the word Marge. Maybe I will just say, 'Hi Toby,' had a good day today, oh by the way, I was chatting to Marge and Hilda today from the laundrette, she happened to mention whether or not they teach sex lessons at school these days."

"Now you are being stupid Rose," said Hilda, just ask what sort of subjects they teach these days, see what he says."

"I'm just going to leave it for now; I'm regretting even starting up this conversation about Toby." Rose finished her brew and quickly turned her attention to an elderly person struggling with the technology of operating a washing machine.

Meanwhile, at Lakeside Secondary School, Toby met up with Liam just outside the school gates as Liam was getting out of his father's car. "Over here Liam," said Toby enthusiastically. Toby wanted to keep his date with Mary quiet until he felt it was developing into something more serious. "Well, I guess you should find out about the selection for the school football team today Toby."

"Yes, I guess so Liam."

"You don't sound too happy Toby; got things on your mind you would like to talk about"

"Na, I'm fine thank you, Liam, just don't want to be disappointed that's all; I know I can play well at times; I just keep getting this funny feeling that I won't be selected, the story of my life."

"What do you mean by that Toby; the story of your life."

"Well, I suppose what I'm saying is, that I must stop feeling sorry for myself all the time; self-pity is something I need to flush out of my system."

"Yeah, you're right Toby, you do. You have a caring and warm family, and also, you have me as your best friend."

"Yeah thanks for that Liam, it means a lot." Deep down inside Toby was burning with pain. Toby has just seen Liam's father dropping Liam off at school, how Toby would long to have his father in his life. Toby love's his mother and sister Holly but has always wondered how his life would have been with a father figure by his side, someone to be there when he needed him. Toby looked up to the heavens for comfort knowing that somewhere in the deep blue sky, his father would be looking down on him. Toby's mind was now working overtime. Who knows what Toby was saying underneath his breath, or what he was thinking when he looked up at the fluffy white clouds, all I can say is, that Toby's life was about to change in a mysterious way.

CHAPTER 2

TOBY'S BIRTHDAY BRINGS A MAGICAL GIFT

It was now getting close to lunch, and Toby and Liam had still not heard anything as to whether or not they had made the school football team. As they were sitting down in the school canteen chit-chatting away between each bite of their sandwiches, they heard someone say. "Thc selection for the school football team is up on the notice board; in the corridor by the headmaster's office."

"Wow!" said Liam, let's go and have a look, Toby."

"Just want to finish off my lunch first Liam, there's no big rush."

"You're not telling me that you can't wait to see if you've made the football team Toby.

"That's exactly what I am saying Liam, we can go when I have finished my lunch."

"Ok Toby, I'll wait until you've finished, just don't take too long about it." Toby decided that he had eaten as much as he could anyway; he had gone right off his food. This was now becoming a habit of Toby's, nerves kicking in, and then not being able to stomach his food. In the corridor there was quite a gathering of lads all hugged together looking for their names. You could hear all sorts of remarks being spouted about: "Didn't make it, I did, I'm on the possible list if someone breaks a leg, useless that one, and how on earth did he get in the team." All these remarks were making Toby feel very anxious and concerned about the outcome. Just as Toby and Liam were getting into striking distance of the notice board, one of the bullies of the school, George Bulldog, grabbed Toby by the collar of his school blazer. Going eye to eye with Toby, George yelled in a growling aggressive voice, "Don't bother checking Travis, you haven't made it, you couldn't get into a primary school football team." This remark had everyone in fits of childish laughter at Toby's expense. Toby sadly just buried his head in shame; he just wanted the ground to open up so he could disappear forever.

"Just get stuffed," said Liam to George, "go and chew on a bone dog face."

"You'll regret you ever said that Fenners, I'll see you after school.

"Yeah, in your dreams dog face, you couldn't fight your way out of a paper bag."

"Don't worry about him Toby, he's just one of those people that sees kindness as a weakness in a person."

"Aren't you scared of him Liam; I've heard he is a bit of a hard nut."

"He probably is Toby, but you can't let people like him run your life. Once they realise you're not scared of them, they tend to leave you alone; anyway, I'm a fast runner; he couldn't even make it to the toilet on time without wetting himself."

"I wish I had your courage," said Toby still laughing at Liam's remark. Liam was a more self-assured person and would always stick up for Toby in his time of need, and didn't take kindly to bullies. Eventually, Toby and Liam got close enough to the notice board. There it was in black and white; Toby unfortunately hadn't made the football team. Toby was gutted even though he half expected it. "Come on Toby," said Liam trying to give him a shoulder to cry on, "I can guarantee you that there will still be more opportunities on the horizon, just because you haven't made the team now doesn't mean you can't get into the team at a later date."

"Let's face it Liam, I'm kidding myself if I think I can make the team; having a pair of football boots of my own would be a good starting point."

Meanwhile, at Lilly Pink School for Girls, it was now common knowledge that Mary and Toby are seeing each other like Boyfriend and girlfriend. Mary was certainly not keeping it quiet. Mary was a popular girl at school just like Liam was at Lakeside, what this meant is, no one was ever going to question her choice of boyfriend, even though Toby was just under a year younger than her. "Are you meeting up with Toby tonight Mary?" asked Lucy enquiringly.

"Well, we have planned to meet up later after school, however, he will find out today if he has made the football team, if he hasn't, then I'm not sure what his emotions are going to be like."

"Football, yuk, not really my thing, I just can't see the fun element in kicking a bag of wind around a football field."

"Well to be fair Lucy, not mine either, however, I was chatting to Toby this morning and he made it sound very interesting."

"Well, if you a get a lad that can convince you that there is more to football than some of us girls think, then you've got yourself a good man there Mary."

Mary laughed out loud, "How right you are Lucy." Just then the bell went for the final lesson of the day. "Catch you later Mary, I will try to phone you."

"Ok Lucy, enjoy your evening, catch you later."

With School now over for the day, Toby had the horrible task of informing all of his close friends and family about not making the school football team. The first port of call would be Archie's' Confectionery where Mary's mum worked part-time. Fortunately, the look on his saddened face, as he walked into the shop, was enough for Mrs Callaghan to realise it wasn't going to be good news. "Not to worry Toby," said Mrs Callaghan, "there'll be other opportunities."

"*Now where have I heard that before?*" said Toby to himself. Toby wanted to hear positive news, something to cheer him up. Just then Mary entered the shop on her way home from school. "Hi Toby," she said with a huge smile.

"Before you ask Mary; no, I didn't make the school football team."

"Aww, no problem Toby, come here and give me a huge hug." Well, that was the tonic Toby needed. Mary wrapped her arms around Toby so tight that he could hardly breathe, not that Toby was complaining. Mary's Mum just looked at her daughter and smiled like only a mother can when she sees her daughter falling in love. Toby was now getting over his disappointment, so after walking Mary home with his bike in hand; telling his mum the disappointing news wasn't going to be an issue. "Toby turned to Mary and planted a kiss on her lips that lasted a good few seconds before coming up for air. "I will catch you later Mary."

"Ok, come round after your tea, maybe around 7 ish, if you are ok with that."

"Yes, that's fine Mary, see you later." Toby opened his front door to be greeted by his Mum. "Didn't make the team mum," said Toby like it didn't matter. Fortunately, Toby was now over all his disappointment and had no problem with the issue, as for his mum; well she had just slipped into a state of mourning at Toby's bad news. "Come here Toby and let me give you a sympathetic hug." Toby's mum had already had a plan in place just in case it was going to be bad news; good forward thinking can prevent disappointment. "Take a seat, Toby, I have something to say." Toby was now feeling alarmed, Toby thought he was in for a 'Birds and Bees' lecture on sexual behaviour, a lecture that he was ill-prepared for.

"I have been thinking Toby. It's your birthday in less than two weeks, and I believe I have come up with a solution to your problem. I know where I can get hold of some football boots for you and they will not cost me a penny. With that in mind, I should be able to afford for you to have a birthday party at our house; you can invite Mary and some of your friends if you like."

"That sounds fantastic Mum, but where are you getting the boots from?"

"Don't you worry about that Toby, just leave everything to me."

"Thank you, Mum, I'm so lucky to have a mother like you, now it's my turn to give you a hug.

Two weeks down the line on the eve of Toby's 14th birthday, Toby's mum unleashed her first surprise on Toby. It was about 8 pm in the evening, Toby had just come back from visiting Mary and their well-developed relationship. Toby's mum sat Toby down knowing that what she was about to say would have to be said very carefully, and in a sensitive manner. Holly, Toby's sister, had already been brought up to speed by her mum on what was going to happen, so kept hidden away in her bedroom.

"Ok Toby, follow me upstairs," said Toby's mum. Toby was none the wiser about what his mum was up to and again was feeling very tense. At the top of the stairs and now standing on the landing, Toby's mum looked up to the attic. "Ok Toby, just pull the ladders down will you, and turn the attic light on."

"What's going on mum?"

"I have a surprise for you in the attic. You go up first Toby and I will follow, mind your head when you stand up Toby."

"Ouch!" said Toby, "thanks for the late warning, Mum.

"Are you ok Toby? It sounded very painful."

"I'll live, just a flesh wound, nothing a good surgeon couldn't put right."

"You shouldn't joke about things like that Toby, even though I thought it was funny."

"Thanks a lot, Mum, I now know who to come to when I want a shoulder to cry on."

"You know I was only messing, Toby." Toby's mum followed Toby into the attic. The attic was dark and cold with not much space to stand up in. "Sit down over there Toby, next to the wooden chest, there is something I need to show you. In this chest are lots of heirlooms that belonged to your father, items that you have never seen before. After your father passed away, I put all his belongings that were precious to me into this chest. I have never opened the chest since the day I closed it some 14 years ago."

"Wow! Are you sure you want to open it mum; you don't have to you know."

"No, I know I don't have to Toby, but I feel it's time for me to try and put the past behind me and get on with my life, I might even keep my eye open for another man. I'm not sure if I am ready for a relationship yet though, maybe if the right man comes along, you never know. Listen to me; If your father could hear me now, I know what he would be saying, '*Go for it Rose if it makes you happy, live your life*.'"

"Mum....what are you going on about," said Toby looking confused.

"Oh, nothing Toby, I am just reminiscing, just thinking about your father. Anyway, ignore what I just said and let's see if I can remember what's inside the chest." The chest was huge, Toby's mum carefully tried to open the weighted lid, it seemed to be stuck down like two heavy magnets were holding the lid together. "I can't understand why it won't open; can you give me a hand Toby; see if you can get it to open." As soon as Toby touched the lid with his delicate hands, it was as if a curse and been lifted from the chest. The lid opened with the ease of a swallow flying in the sky. "Did you hear that Mum?"

"Hear what Toby." Feeling a little scared by what he had heard, Toby explained. "I heard a voice and."

"And what Toby, and what?"

"I heard like a whoosh of air escaping from the chest."

"I never heard a thing," said Toby's mum. Toby and his mum were now looking around the attic with their heads turning almost 360 degrees. "Are you absolutely sure you heard nothing Mum?"

"Well unless I'm going deaf, and you never know at my age, like I said, I never even heard a whisper."

"It was probably nothing Mum, just my imagine nation running away with me." Toby and his mum started to sieve through his father's belongings. First of all, they found a photo of his father in a small golden frame, a frame that housed a beautiful portrait-size photo. "Mum, can I have this photo mum to put in my bedroom?" said Toby staring at the photo and holding it with a vice-like grip.

"Of course you can Toby, your father would like that. And what have we here? It's your father's wristwatch; the one I bought for your father's 40th birthday." Toby could see his mum's eyes filling up with tears as the reminiscing continued.

"Don't cry mum, I miss him too you know; for some reason not known to myself, I always get the feeling he is here with us, the feeling that he is out there somewhere watching over me."

"Yes, I know what you mean, I get the same feeling too Toby, he may not be able to show himself as we know him, but he will always be here in spirit." Toby's mum gave Toby a hug and wrapped her arm around his shoulder to comfort herself as well as comforting Toby. With the tears now gone it was back to the chest: Wedding ring, Favourite mug, Celtic Thunder CD, Baseball Cap, and then best of all, the reason why the chest was opened. "What have we here Toby?" His mum pulled out a pair of football boots that looked like they were from WWI. "These boots have been passed down from generation to generation Toby, and I would like you to have them."

The look on Toby's face said it all, was he supposed to feel happy and thrilled, should he feel disappointed that he would face more embarrassment and cruelty from people like George Bulldog, I don't think Toby knew how to feel.

"Wonderful mum," said Toby fibbing, "thank you so much. I'll show all the doubters how to play football now, you wait and see." Sometimes a little white lie can be of more comfort than the truth, but not always recommended. Toby's mum was so happy that Toby liked his WWI football boots, and not only that, he still had his party to look forward to.

Toby passed the football boots to his mother along with the picture frame that housed his father's photo. With the chest now closed and the attic stairs put away, Toby made his way into his bedroom. Toby placed the photo of his father on his bedside cabinet in a position that meant that he could see his father before going to sleep, and also, so he could see the photo when he woke up in the morning. He also carefully placed the WWI football boots on the floor by his bed; maybe hoping that the Tooth Fairy would take them away in the night.

That night something strange happened. After going to sleep, Toby was woken up by the sound of a ghostly voice, the voice that he had heard earlier in the attic; it was as if there was a presence in the room. Toby was tossing and turning all night until eventually he couldn't sleep anymore. Toby decided to get out of the warmth of his bed and make his way downstairs to get a drink, at the same time still feeling concerned about the voice he heard. "What's going on?" said Toby's mum who was now awake.

"Nothing mum, just couldn't sleep, I need a drink."

"Well hurry up and then get yourself back into bed, it's 4 am in the morning, Oh and by the way, happy birthday Toby, see you in a few hours."

"Thank you, Mum," said Toby. As morning dawned, Toby turned his bedside light on and rushed out of bed to find that his WWI footy boots had somehow done a lap of his bed space, and the photo of his father was lying face down on the floor. At first, Toby thought no more about it, maybe he had knocked the photo off in the night, and possibly kicked the boots while getting back into bed. Toby just picked up the photo and placed it back onto his bedside cabinet; as far as the boots were concerned, I think Toby would have been more than happy for them to have disappeared out of the room. With Toby now so excited for the day that lay ahead, everything that went on last night was now history.

Toby still had his paper round to do before breakfast to his annoyance, however, with the excitement of knowing it was his birthday, Toby did his paper round in super quick time; he just wanted to get home to be with his family. On return, Toby made his way upstairs into his bedroom to get ready for school. Before Toby could even put a sentence together his sister Holly came into his bedroom to give him a huge hug and wish him a happy birthday. "Happy birthday little brother," she said excitedly! "I have got you a birthday card and a small gift for being such a wonderful brother."

"Aww, thank you, Holly, you are so kind." Holly stayed until Toby had unwrapped his present, she just couldn't wait to see the look on his face. It was a beautiful leather wallet that Toby was overwhelmed with.

"I know you are earning your own money from your paper round, so I thought you would now have somewhere to put your money, it might help you to save as well."

"Wow! I love it, thank you again, Holly, it's a very thoughtful gift." It was now time for Toby to get washed and dressed before making his way downstairs. "Breakfast is ready Toby," shouted his mum from the foot of the stairs.

"On my way now Mum." Minutes later Toby made his way into the kitchen area where he was greeted by his mum.

"Happy 14th birthday Toby, I have got you a small gift to open Toby; I couldn't not get you anything even though I am paying for your party."

"There was no need mum, really, you didn't need to get me anything." Toby's mum handed over a box that was about 18 inches square. "Go on Toby, open it up." With Holly now in attendance, the unwrapping began. With the wrapping paper now gone, the box was exposed. It was just a case of getting it open. It was a top-of-the-range size 5 international football; now if the boots were going to be an embarrassment, then this football was certainly going to be the envy of his friends. Toby gave his mum a huge hug once more, the second of the day. Unfortunately, all this excitement had once more cost Toby his appetite. Toby's mum was having a day off from the Launderette with so much to arrange for Toby's party. Hilda and Marge had baked the most wonderful cake for Toby, a cake that Toby knows nothing about; it just needed collecting. "Are you off to school now Toby," said his mum, trying to get him out of the house and from underneath her feet.

"Yes, just waiting on Mary, she should be here in a minute." Just then Toby caught a glimpse of her coming up his driveway from the window. "I'm off now mum, see you later." Toby's mum glanced out of the window to see her son for one last time; a peck on the cheek had now turned into a full-blown snog in just two weeks, thus causing Toby's mum to smile. I suppose it was part of Toby's birthday present from Mary. The first port of call for Rose was the Launderette to pick up the cake; not knowing what to expect, Rose was knocked out by how beautiful the cake looked. "You have done an amazing job, Toby will be so pleased, I can't wait to see the look on his face," said Rose.

"We thought that putting a bike as the centre piece of the cake would be fitting," said Hilda, "you know, with the fact he does a paper round."

"Aww, you think of everything don't you, I absolutely love it. How much do I owe you, Marge, and Hilda?"

"Don't be daft Rose, you owe us nothing; tell Toby it's a present from Hilda and me."

"Thank you so much; where would I be without friends."

"How is the relationship between Toby and Mary developing Rose?"

"Well Hilda, let's just say they are getting on swimmingly."

"So pleased said Marge."

"Mary will be coming to Toby's party tonight, and again, let's just say, I will be keeping a close eye on them; without being too intrusive of course."

"Well naturally Rose, of course, you will," said Hilda sarcastically.

"Listen up you pair, it's been lovely chatting to you both, but I must get a move on now; so much to do. I will catch you all tomorrow and let you know how it went, bye for now." Rose had a list as long as your arm but managed to get through it all by the end of the day.

Toby was quite amazed when he entered his house after coming home from school to see the effort his mum had made; along with Mary's mum and a little help from Bob and Brenda next door. The house was entertainingly fully decked out now with all sorts of surprises: Sandwiches, Cakes, Sausage rolls, Balloons of plenty, it was far more than Toby could have ever wished for. It was now getting close to zero hour; the time when Toby would be welcoming his guests. Mary was the first guest to arrive; straight up to Toby's bedroom she went under the scrutiny of Rose, to make sure Toby was looking his best. One by one the guests arrived including Toby's best friend Liam Fenwick, and Mary's best friend Lucy; all in all, there were about 20 of Toby's friends and family. Toby's wallet was bulging with notes, most of the guests found it easier to put some money in a birthday card as opposed to buying a gift; you didn't find Toby complaining. Toby is a guy that is easily pleased; just having his friends around him would have been enough for Toby to enjoy the party. Toby did get one special gift though; from who else but Mary. Mary decided to get Toby on his own before giving him her present. Mary handed over a small box wrapped in beautiful wrapping paper. "Go on Toby open it," said Mary eagerly.

"You shouldn't have Mary; I've only been going out with you for two weeks, surely that doesn't warrant a gift."

"You're not getting away with that feeble excuse Toby Travis, it's your birthday, it's a day when you should get spoiled, now open it." Toby was all fingers and thumbs until finally, he saw the most decorative box. "Open it up then Toby." Inside the box was a stunning gold necklace chain. Toby was overwhelmed by Mary's kind gift. "May I have the pleasure of putting it around your neck Toby?"

"Yes please," said Toby, "just make sure you don't choke me though."

"Don't be silly Toby, I will be really gentle with you; the pleasure will be all mine." Mary started to place the chain around Toby's neck in a seductive manner with her sensitive fingers. God knows what Rose would have said if she had seen Mary putting the necklace around Toby's neck the way she was doing. The deed was now done; Mary and Toby reunited themselves with the party. During the next hour, Toby got chatting to Liam. "Liam," shouted Toby, "I want to show you something in my bedroom."

"Not sure I like the sound of that Toby."

"Nothing like that Liam, anyway I have a girlfriend, and I am sure Mary would have something to say about it."

"Ok Toby, just making sure." Liam now felt safe to follow Toby into his bedroom after the reassurance from Toby.

"My mum has bought me some football boots; well let's just say they are hand-downs, two generations I think," said Toby.

"Well let's have a look then Toby." Toby showed Liam the boots and at the same time sat eagerly waiting for Liam's response.

"So, what do you think? And please don't beat around the bush, just tell me honestly what you think, also remember, you're my friend."

"Honestly speaking Toby, Ouch, do they actually fit?"

"You know what, I'm not sure, not tried them on yet, I think they date back to WWI" That remark had Liam in fits of laughter, he just couldn't contain himself as he spilled over onto the floor.

"I'm so sorry Toby, I'm not laughing at you or the boots, it's just the way you said WWI."

"No worries, I shall have to tell my mum that they don't fit, I'll tell her they're too small"

"Well, at least you can try them on Toby, see if they'll fit."

"Can't do any harm I suppose, actually, they do look too small. Oh well, here we go. Wow! They fit like a glove, to be perfectly honest though Liam, they look more like a glove than a boot." Toby got his football out, the one his mum had bought for him. Now that was a head-turner for Liam, "Wow! What a great football, can I have a kick, Toby?"

"Yes, but be careful not to break anything, I don't think my mum would be best pleased." Liam did a few small but delicate kicks against the wall before handing the ball back to Toby. "Let's see what you can do with your new boots," said Liam. Toby drew back his right foot expecting to tap the ball to Liam, 'Wrong!' The power he hit the ball with had Liam running for cover.

"Holy mackerel Toby, not so hard, you scared me to death."

"I only tapped it with the outside of my foot."

"Well if that was a tap, what do you think you would be like on a football field?"

"We may never know, with the fact that I don't plan on wearing them."

"Well, that's your choice, Toby, I'll tell you what though, on the subject of football, do you fancy a game at the weekend; it's at the local park on Saturday? You can play in the team that I have put together, most of them are from our school; we are playing against some of the lads from Mall Bank School, you'll have no excuses now.

"What! You expect me to wear these WWI boots," said Toby, "that'll be a great laugh for everyone at my expense; somehow I don't think so Liam."

"I'll tell you what Toby, I will bring a spare pair of my boots if you like, but bring yours along just in case I forget."

"Ok, what time does it start then Liam?"

"11 in the morning, best if you try to be there for about 10.45 for a warm-up."

"That's settled then, I think we better go and join the rest of your friends before they send out a search party." Once back downstairs, Liam bumped into Holly, who to be truthfully honest, found Holly very attractive. "So you are Holly, I've heard so much about you from Toby," said Liam in a flirtatious kind of way.

"Don't believe a word he says, if you do, then this conversation is over."

"Ok, but he did say you were kind of a generous and fun-loving person, and that he was proud to have you as a sister."

"Oh, then yes, believe every word he said, it's all true. Normally I don't admit to being his sister, especially when he is being a pain in the backside; truthfully though, I think the world of him. It hasn't been easy for both of us to lose our father when we did."

"Yes, I did hear Holly, so sorry about that."

"I'm not looking for any sympathy, anyway that's enough of that, what about you, tell me something about yourself."

"Yeah, you're right Holly. My name is Liam, Liam Fenwick, Toby's very close friend, but I only admit it if he is behaving himself, if he's misbehaving, then I say I have never heard of him. Holly was almost doubled over with tears of laughter; she was finding Liam's sense of humour very appealing.

"So funny Liam, my sides are aching with laughter,"

"So, you go to the Lilly Pink School then do you, Holly?"

"Yes, that's correct, two more years then I will be leaving."

"Just one more year for me; then maybe I will go to uni," said Liam. Holly and Liam were getting on like a house in fire, well at least for now, who knows what might happen in the future.

It was now close to 10 o'clock and everyone had gone home. "Off to bed now mum," said Toby, "thank you for a wonderful day."

"I'm so glad you enjoyed it, Toby."

"It was the best mum, thanks again."

"Ok, Toby; sleep tight, don't let the bed bugs bite." Toby was now sitting on the edge of his bed looking at the photo of his dad and sending a goodnight text to Mary on his phone. Within minutes, Toby was away with the fairies. It must have been close to midnight when Toby was woken up once more by the same sound he heard the night before, however, instead of going downstairs, Toby this time decided to brave it out as he sat up in bed. There was silence for a few minutes until the ghostly noise came back even louder. "Toby, Toby," could be heard around the room. Toby froze for a minute only to hear the photo of his dad falling on the floor. "Whose there?" asked Toby who was now feeling petrified, "please go away you're scaring me." Suddenly a ghostly transparent figure could be seen at the end of Toby's bed, the outline of a person could clearly be seen; seconds later it was clear that it was Toby's father. Toby was now transfixed and couldn't move his body.

"Toby, Toby, it's me your father, please don't be afraid, I love you, Toby."

Toby was now in a state of shock. "Dad, Is that you Dad?"

"Yes Toby, it's me," said his dad with an air of ghostly timbre. "Two nights ago, when you were in the attic with your mum, and your mum said she had a surprise for you; well do you remember when you opened the chest?"

"Yes, I remember very well. Mum was really struggling to open it; she asked me to help her."

"And then what happened?"

"Well, as soon as I touched the lid, it just opened on its own, I didn't have to use any force at all."

"Go on then Toby, what happened next?"

"Well, I remember hearing a whoosh kind of noise, and like a cold draft that brushed over my body; it was like the rising of a spirit. I asked my mum if she heard the noise and also, did she feel the cold air that I felt."

"And did she?"

"Well, sadly she said no, she didn't feel or hear anything."

"Well, that night, because it was you that opened the chest, you let my spirit out Toby; you have allowed me to move freely in the land of the living dead." Toby was finding this all too much to understand; it was far too much information for Toby to take in. "Wow! It's really you Dad isn't it."

"Yes Toby, it's really me. From now on I can come and see you whenever I please, and if you ever need me, you can call me." Toby was still trying to get his head around this extraordinary spiritual thing when his dad gave him more concern to be alarmed.

"I see that you have a beautiful girlfriend, Mary from next door." Feeling worried about his father's remark Toby replied. "How do you know that Dad?"

"I can see everything you do and get up to Toby, let's just say, it's one of the perks of the job."

"Perks of the job Dad, what do you mean by that? You don't see everything we do, do you, Dad?"

"No Toby, even us spirits show some discretion. However, Toby, I've seen that you are struggling with your football. You must wear the boots that your mum gave you Toby; they are full of magic to the person they belong to."

"Magic, you are making no sense Dad."

"Then let me enlighten you, Toby. Without the boots, you will continue to struggle and perform, wear the boots, and you will perform like a professional."

"People will laugh at me Dad; I can see it now as I run onto the field"

"Let them laugh Toby, he who laughs last, laughs longest, you will do well to remember those valuable words."

"Can I speak to you tomorrow Dad?"

"Now that's a good question, Toby, of course you can, we spirits are very discreet; as I said, we come and go like ships in the night." Suddenly the spirit became weak and translucent, it vanished before Toby's eyes and before he could get the answer he was searching for. With the spirit now gone, Toby tried to get some welcomed sleep but without too much success; about 3 or four hours was all that Toby got that night. In the morning Toby's mum noticed that Toby was looking worse for wear. "Are you ok Toby?" asked his mum looking concerned.

"Yes, fine mum," answered Toby not wanting to say anything about his conversation with his father.

"Did your Paper round go ok?"

"Yes Mum, it did go ok. Why am I getting the third degree, why are you asking me all these questions?"

"Sorry, Mr Grumpy, just making sure you're ok."

"I'm not grumpy Mum, just a little tired." Toby's mum was thinking, *maybe all the emotions from last night are kicking in, a bit like a hangover for adults.* No more was said. On the way to school, Toby asked Mary if she would like to pop around that evening.

"Yes sure Toby, any reason, even though I will look forward to it."

"I have something I would like to discuss with you, but it will be our secret Mary and no one else's."

"Ok," said Mary looking mystified, "can I have a clue what it's about?"

"Not really Mary, there is just something I need to ask you in private." Just then Mary's bus arrived. "See you tonight Mary."

"Well do I get a kiss Toby boy or not?" said Mary feeling a little dejected.

"Yes of course Mary, sorry, I was just thinking about something else."

"Not other girls I hope, you're mine to keep, no one else is having you."

"Don't be daft Mary, catch you later." Mary couldn't wait for the evening to arrive, and at the same time, she needed to talk to her best friend Lucy. It must have been lunchtime before Mary managed to meet up with Lucy. "Did you get my text, Lucy?"

"Yes, what's the problem?" said Lucy.

"Toby, that's the problem, Lucy. He is acting very abnormal and saying strange things."

"He's acting like what Mary? I'm not sure I know what you're on about?"

"Like he wants to meet me this evening at his house, he said he has something to tell me in private."

"Wow!" gasps Lucy, "things are moving on quickly."

"No, I'm sure it's nothing like that, I'm at a loss Lucy; I will just have to wait until tonight."

"Maybe he wants to take the relationship to the next level."

"No, not Toby, he's too nice and respectful for that. We have only been seeing each other for just over 3 weeks, hardly long enough for us to get to know each other."

"You must keep me up to date with the entire goings on Mary, I'm so intrigued."

Back at the Lakeside Secondary School, the news that Toby will be playing in Liam's football team on Saturday is doing the rounds. George Bulldog couldn't resist a snipe at Toby as he stood almost nose to nose with Toby snarling through his teeth.

"You're a dead man tomorrow Travis, I wouldn't bother turning up if I were you."

"Well if you are trying to intimidate me, then it's working, maybe I won't turn up." George just pushed Toby aside as if to say, "You're in my way Travis, get out of my space." All this again brought fits of laughter from George's small but nasty army of boys. Was this the final straw for Toby? Would Toby turn up for the game tomorrow or not? And had George finally got to Toby? Toby had some big decisions to make that could affect the rest of his life.

CHAPTER 3

MAKE OR BREAK

That evening, Mary arrived unexpectedly earlier than planned, her eagerly awaited anticipation of what Toby wanted to see her about had got the better of her.

"Toby, Mary's here," yelled Toby's mum from the foot of the stairs.

"Two minutes Mum, just finishing off something."

"Oh just go up Mary, save hanging around, he says two minutes, what he really means is, I will be about 15 minutes."

"Ok thank you Mrs Travis." As Mary dashed up the stairs to Toby's bedroom, she noticed that Toby's door was ajar. Typical Mary was still feeling puzzled about what Toby wanted to talk about; so what came next was going to be a surprise for her and Toby. Mary couldn't for one minute ever imagine what she was about to set her eyes on. Mary got a right eye full of Toby's backside as he stood there naked and proud as proud could be, but more was to come. Mary yelled out, "Oh my giddy aunt," at the same time covering her mouth with her hand, it was quite inevitable that Toby's first reaction would be to turn around without even thinking that Mary would be standing there.

"Mary, cover your eyes," yelled Toby as he hurriedly tried to find something suitable to cover up his scrawny body. Mary did as she was told covering her eyes with her hand, well at least that's what Toby was hoping; Mary couldn't resist a slight peep through her semi-closed fingers. Toby wrapped a towel around the bottom half of his body and apologised to Mary. "Don't apologise Toby," said Mary feeling embarrassed, "it was my fault, I should have knocked."

"Well it's over and done with now; just take a seat on the bed Mary while I get dressed." In a strange sort of way, Mary felt more comfortable with the situation; it was going to happen at some time in their relationship, even at their young age. Mary and Toby were both level-headed kids that were growing up fast. One day you're a child without a care in the world, and then, well before you know it, puberty sets in and you become an adult with responsibilities.

While Toby was getting dressed, Mary couldn't stop herself from texting Lucy. Unfortunately, Mary only managed to tell Lucy half of her story before Toby was fully dressed. Lucy was now feeling concerned about the vague text she received, the text that said Mary had just seen Toby naked. With Toby now sitting next to Mary on the edge of the bed, all that could be heard was a continuous buzzing from Mary's phone; text after text from Lucy until Toby thought it would be a good idea to turn her phone off. Toby didn't know how to start this unusual conversation as Mary waited eagerly for him to start. "Do you believe in life after death Mary, you know, spirits and things, reincarnation?"

"Not really Toby, the only spirit I know is my dad's whiskey.

"Now you're being silly Mary, you know what I am talking about has absolutely nothing at all to do with whiskey."

"Well, if you are on about ghosts and things, then I would say I would be sitting on the fence, I really don't know; seeing is believing is my motto, I would have to see one to convince myself ghosts exist"

"So, if a spirit was to show itself, you know, in like a human form in this room tonight, would you then believe in Ghosts?"

"What are you trying to say, Toby?"

"Well, it's just like you said Mary, and I agree with you, you have to see something to believe in it."

"Then I guess, yes, I believe I would. Where is this conversation going Toby, I'm feeling a little concerned?"

"Well last night Mary, around Midnight, a spirit came into my room.

"Ok, just stop there Toby, are you trying to tell me that a spirit came into your room last night?"

"Yes, however, just let me finish what I was trying to say, Mary. I was woken up by a ghostly voice and the sound of my father's photo falling off my bedside cabinet and onto the floor."

"You must have been imagining it, Toby, maybe you were just having a really bad dream, a nightmare, or something like that."

"No, it wasn't a dream Mary, or a nightmare; I remember visibly seeing my father at the end of my bed, and then talking to him. I knew you wouldn't believe me, Mary, in fact, to be perfectly honest; I'm not sure whether I believe it now, you've got me doubting myself."

"I am not saying I don't believe you, Toby, it's just a difficult thing to imagine. People do say they have seen Ghosts, so it's not beyond the realms of possibility that it could have happened."

"Well, this is why I brought you here tonight Mary; I wanted to see if my father will show himself again, just like last night. Do you think your mum and dad will allow you to sleep over in my room tonight?

"Did I hear you correctly Toby, sleep over, as in sleep in your room?"

"Yes, you heard me correctly Mary, is that a problem."

"Well not for me, I'm just thinking what my mum and dad might say, and also your mum. I do have a sleeping bag I can use; I suppose I can sleep on the floor, and also there's no school tomorrow; what about your paper round?"

"Saturday is my day off from delivering papers so it will work for me."

"Ok, I will phone my mum now, see what she says."

After shrewdly exploiting her parent's good faith in their amazingly beautiful good-looking daughter, who wouldn't do anything to defame the good name of the Callaghan household, her parents agreed it would be fine for her to sleep over. Toby's mum was more relaxed with the situation and could see absolutely no reason at all for them to sleep in the same room; with certain restrictions in place of course. Mary trundled off to get her belongings and then within ten minutes arrived back with her sleeping bag and overnight bag.

"Can I use the bathroom to get changed into my pyjamas Toby?"

"No, I'm afraid not, you can get changed here in my bedroom in front of me Mary; after all you have seen my body."

"Toby Travis I am shocked, are you being serious."

"Don't be ridiculous Mary," of course you can use the bathroom. Well to be perfectly honest Mary, I don't think your parents would be too pleased if you got changed in my bedroom, do you?'

"Well they are not here are they?"

"No they are not Mary; now get into the bathroom and get changed."

"I will get changed in front of you if you want me to Toby, like you said; I have seen your body."

"Mary, I was joking, now go and get changed in the bathroom before you get me into trouble; it's just across the landing, right in front of you." On return, Mary rolled her sleeping bag out on the floor next to Toby's bed. "Will you be ok there Mary, it's not too uncomfortable, is it?"

"No, it's not uncomfortable Toby; I'll be fine; I just need a pillow to rest my head on."

"Here, you can use one of mine," catch," said Toby.

"Ouch, that hit me in the face Toby, you bully."

"Don't be such a drama queen Mary."

"Drama Queen, you called me a Drama Queen, do it again and I will have to tell my mum that you found your way into my sleeping bag during the night."

"Don't you dare Mary; don't even joke about things like that." Toby and Mary were now ready in all respects for what lay ahead. "I'm feeling tired now Toby, I think I will try and get some sleep, what time is it?"

"10.30, yeah, I think I will get some shut-eye too. I have a football match tomorrow at the park at 11 am, do you fancy coming along to watch Mary?"

"I would love to Toby; I will cheer you on."

"All that said Mary, I'm not too sure if I want to play."

"Why did you say it like you weren't looking forward to it, what's the issue?"

"It's that George Bulldog; he said some spiteful things to me today, saying you're a dead man when I get you on the field tomorrow Travis."

"How dare he say such malicious things, you will play tomorrow Toby; I hope you run rings around him."

"Not much chance of that Mary, George may be a bully, but he can certainly play football."

"Anyway, let's get some sleep; it's almost 11 pm now, goodnight Toby."

"Goodnight Mary."

It was now close to midnight, and Mary was either fast asleep or in a coma, as for Toby, well Toby could be heard snoring by his next-door neighbours Bob and Brenda. Apart from Toby's snoring, there was total silence all around the room. Toby started to fidget as if someone or something was telling him to wake up, just like the other night. Then suddenly, 'BANG!' The photo frame landed on the floor. Toby shot bolt upright in his bed at the same time calling quietly to Mary. "Mary, Mary are you awake? It's started again, wake up Mary." Toby started shaking Mary's sleeping bag until he heard her stir. "Yes, I am now, what's up Toby, what has started again?"

"The photo frame has fallen on the fall, just like last night Mary. "Mary's attention was now forthcoming. Mary crawled out of her sleeping bag dressed in her flower-patterned cotton pyjamas and rubbed her sleepy eyes. "Can I get into bed with you Toby? I feel scared."

"Yes of course Mary, just slowly pull back the quilt Mary and slide under the quilt."

"Give me your hand Toby, I will feel a lot more comfortable holding your hand. So what happens next?"

"I'm not sure Mary; I guess we just have to wait."

"Maybe it's because I am here with you that the spirit won't appear."

"You could be right Mary." Toby and Mary were just staring into oblivion when all of a sudden Toby heard his father's voice once more. Mary was now heading underneath the quilt at a speed more suited to a racing car before Toby reassured her and told her not to be scared. "Mary, get yourself from underneath the quilt, will you? How are you going to see anything from there?" Mary gingerly poked her head out from underneath the quilt, at the same time, ready to dive back under if necessary. With Mary now grasping the end of the quilt with a vice-like grip, a ghostly image appeared at the end of Toby's bed. "Don't scream Mary, just stay calm." Seconds later the transparent image was plain to see, it was Toby's father. Toby's father's voice was now sounding more human and not the ghostly sound we associate with ghosts. It was as if he was still in the land of the living. "What should I say?" asked Mary who was stuck for words for a change.

"Hello would be nice," said Toby's father, in a kind of comical way.

"Oh sugar, he spoke to me, Toby."

"Yes I did," said Toby's father, "just call me Mr Travis or Tom, I don't mind which, Toby, you can call me Dad." The way Toby's father was chatting to them, made Toby and most of all Mary, feel really at home. Nothing like they were expecting.

"Will I be able to speak to you every night?" said Toby.

"Only if I'm not busy, I have my own life to lead now Toby... life, what a laugh, I mean in the world of the living dead. If I can see you need guidance or help, I will pay you a visit, remember what I said Toby, I can see you all the time."

"All the time, what does he mean all the time?" Said Mary looking towards Toby.

"Don't worry Mary, spirits use discretion, isn't that correct Dad?"

"Yes Toby, you learn fast."

"What does your father mean by that Toby?" asked Mary.

"Oh, nothing Mary, just something he said last night."

"Toby, I hear you are playing football tomorrow, and you were thinking of not playing. You must Toby; don't be bullied into not playing. I sadly heard what George was saying to you today. Don't forget your boots Toby; remember what I said about your boots."

"What does your father mean, don't forget your boots Toby?" said Mary.

"Nothing really Mary, my mother got me some boots that use to belong to my Great Grandfather, my Grandfather, and then my father, you could say they have seen better days." Before Toby could say goodbye to his father or ask any more questions; his father wilted away, back to the land of the living dead. Toby turned his bedside light on to provide some welcome light. "Wow! Toby, I just can't believe that I have had a conversation with your father, this sort of thing just doesn't happen. Where are the boots your father was on about Toby? Can I see them?"

"Here they are Mary." Mary was giving them a full inspection, what she was looking for is anyone's business. "They look a little bit dated don't they Toby?"

"Yes Mary, that's because they are a bit dated; it is what has known in the trade as antique."

"Antique? That sounds like they could be worth a few quid Toby."

"A bob or two, you could not give them away Mary. Anyway, let's get some sleep, I've got a long day tomorrow."

"Would you like me to sleep in your bed, Toby?"

"Yes, but somehow, I don't think that's the best idea you have ever come up with, I'll settle for a kiss and a cuddle Mary." A quick kiss and a cuddle and what the butler saw, was as far as it went. Mary slightly reluctantly crawled back into her sleeping bag as Toby turned the light off. Morning arrived as quickly as you could say Jack Frost; you could hear Toby's mum making breakfast, and Toby's sister Holly in the bathroom. "You'll have to wait a moment for the bathroom Mary, Holly is in there; I'm sure she will be out soon." Just then the bathroom door opened. "Bathrooms free now Toby," cried Holly. Just as Holly was entering her bedroom, she saw what she believed to be the back end of a girl closing the bathroom door behind her. Holly was now putting 2 and 2 together and coming up with 5. She immediately made her way to Toby's room for some answers. "Toby, what's going on?" said Holly sternly.

"Sorry, what are you talking about Holly? What do you mean, what's going on? There's nothing going on."

"Did I or did I not just see a girl entering the bathroom,"

"Yes, but there's no need to get your knickers in a twist Holly, it's not what you're thinking."

"Did she sleep in your bedroom last night?"

"Oh, well yes, maybe it is what you were thinking," said Toby like he was a naughty boy.

"So I suppose you going to tell me now she didn't sleep in your bed, and not only that, does mum know?"

"Just let me explain Holly, the rest of it is definitely not what you were thinking," Toby explained to Holly about the sleeping arrangements, but that's about as far as his explaining went; the rest can wait for another day. Holly was now satisfied with the explanation and the fact that her mum knew. "You won't see me bringing lads back Toby, I have standards. Anyway, I need to have a chat with you later, In Private Toby."

"Ok Holly, no problem. If you're around today, I've got a football match later at 11 am at the park, be nice to have some support, maybe it will be a good opportunity for you to have a chat with Mary."

"So, Mary's coming is she, yes I think that would be a good idea, Toby, I would like to get to know her better, and see what she has to say for herself." As Mary was exiting the bathroom, Holly approached her. "Hi Mary, I see you stayed over last night, did you sleep well?"

"Er, yes thank you, I slept on the floor in my sleeping bag."

"Yes I know, Toby as already explained what the sleeping arrangements were, I don't need to hear it all again, I will see you later at the football match, we can get to know each other a lot better," snarled Holy with a disgruntled stare.

"Yes, that would be nice, thank you, I look forward to it." Holly made her way downstairs to chat with her mum. In the meantime, Mary needed to get her story straight with Toby. "I'm not too concerned about what you say to Holly Mary, just don't mention anything about my father; I need to keep it quiet, well at least until I feel the time is right to mention it to Holly," said Toby.

"I won't tell a soul Toby, mum's the word." Meanwhile, back at the corner shop, Mary's mum was chatting to the owner 'Archie Hampson,' about Mary staying over at Toby's house. "Such a lovely boy is Toby, it's a shame that he lost his father even before he was born; we all need a father figure in our life. It was his birthday the other day, I believe he got some football boots from Rose his mother." Just then, the shop bell rang, it was Toby. "Hello Toby," said Mrs Callaghan, "we were just talking about you; were your ears burning?"

"Absolutely on fire Mrs Callaghan, hope it was all good."

"Of course, it was all good Toby, I was just telling Mr Hampson about how pleased I am that Mary has found herself a wonderful level-headed boyfriend."

"Really, I thought she was going out with me, who's the other guy you're referring to?"

"Oh Toby, you do make me laugh, you know what I mean. Mary said she really enjoyed staying over at your house last night and would love to do it again sometime."

"Yes that would be really nice, and thank you for allowing Mary to stay over." Toby was trying to be careful in what he said, the last thing he wanted now was for Mrs Callaghan to find out about the rest of the evening. "I just came in to buy a bottle of Orange Juice, I have a football match in about 20 minutes' time so need to get a move on."

" Of course Toby, here you are, here is your orange juice. Mary did mention this morning that she is going along to watch you play. Well don't let me keep you Toby, see you later, and good luck."

"Thank you so much." Toby got on his bike and was now just minutes away from the park feeling nervous. On arrival, Toby noticed that there was quite a gathering of people doing all sorts of activities at the park; maybe some of them were there to watch the footy game. "Toby, over here," said a familiar voice." It was Liam, Liam Fenwick.

"Hi Liam, how's it going?"

"Fine thanks," said Liam, "Just limbering up, stretching my muscles, don't want to get cramp. Get yourself inside the pavillion Toby and get changed into your kit, here's your shirt, catch." Toby caught his Green and White vertical stripe football shirt and made his way into the changing rooms, followed closely by Liam. "I have brought my spare pair of boots Toby, if you want to try them on."

"Can't be any worse than the pair I've got, just look at the state of these."

"Well I'm trying not to laugh, but yes, I'm afraid on this occasion I will have to agree with you, Toby."

"Cheers Liam, you didn't have to agree with me, kick a man while he's down why don't you."

" Just messing, listen, Toby, whatever boots you choose to wear is fine by me, it's your choice. As soon as you are changed I will get everyone together for a tactical team talk. Toby got changed and instead of putting his father's boots on as his father suggested, Toby made a decision to put Liam's spare pair of more fashionable boots on. "Ok everyone," yelled Liam, "gather around. Liam read out the riot act as well as the team sheet including a couple of substitutes. "Toby, you will be one of my substitutes, I will bring you on for the second half unless someone gets injured, then you will have to come on earlier."

Liam explained the tactics they would be using; although it was only a friendly, Liam was determined to win the match. "Outside now lads, let's go." All the boys were now raring to go, exchanging aggressive verbals with each other as they exited the changing room.

"Toby, just a quick word," said Liam, "I am not expecting too much from my team, however, I hope we can put on an impressive performance, then who knows, we might win. I shall be playing you anywhere on the field where we need a position filling; enjoy the game, and don't worry about George who is playing for the other team, I'll take care of him. There's a bench by the side of the pitch, just take a seat there until half time then make your way back into the changing room." Just then Toby noticed Mary and Holly standing by the edge of the football pitch hoping to get a glimpse of him. "Where's Toby?" asked Mary, "I can't see him anywhere."

"I'm not sure," said Holly, looking over toward the pitch. "There he is, over on that bench Mary."

Mary not being too conversant with the game asked Holly what he was doing over there. "I think it means he is being used as a substitute. They will bring him on later when he is needed, or something like that, something to do with tactics I think. Anyway, Mary, I think we need to have a little chat don't you?"

"Yes of cause Holly," said Mary expecting to be told that there is no Santa Claus, there is no Tooth Fairy and a Stork brings babies speech. Although Mary was the same age as Holly, to Holly it didn't mean a fig; Toby was her brother and she was just looking out for him like a good sister should. The game kicked off with excitement for Mary; watching her first-ever football game was something she was looking forward to. "So where do you see your relationship with Toby going Mary?"

"Well, if you're asking me do I love him, I guess the answer is yes."

"And, do you see your relationship with Toby going to a higher plane?"

"I'm not sure, again if you're asking me do I find Toby sexually attractive, then yes; the answer to your question would be yes."

"So, does that answer confirm my worst fears that you have slept with him, Mary?"

"Well, the look on your face Holly right now is telling me that that is what you are thinking. Last night we shared Toby's bed for about 5 minutes, fully clothed may I add, I think that should give you your answer Holly." Mary was giving as good as she got, she was the sort of girl that certainly wouldn't be classed as a doormat; no one was going to walk over her. This sort of remark without doubt had Holly smirking.

"All of a sudden Mary and Holly's attention was drawn to the football pitch. Goal!" could be heard from across the park.

"What the hell was all that about Holly?" asked Mary looking puzzled.

"5 minutes into the game and the other team have scored a goal; that means Lakeside School is losing the match by 1 goal to nil."

"They need to get Toby on to the pitch Holly, he'll show them."

"I do like you Mary, and I am sorry for all the questions, I just need to be sure for Toby's sake that your relationship is not going t be a one-week wonder; he's not had it easy you know, you turning up has been a revelation, the best thing that could have happened to him, I've never seen him so happy."

"Pardon me for being frank Mary, but do you have any plans on sleeping with Toby in the future?"

"Well pardon me for saying, it's certainly none of your business Holly. How dare you ask such a pertinent question? However, I will not shy away from the question. Yes, I believe I would if Toby was comfortable with it, of course, I would. Toby is the best thing that has happened to me as well Holly. It's been three weeks now, so I guess it's definitely not a one-week wonder to answer one of your other questions." Not only was Toby's and Mary's relationship blooming, but Mary and Holly were certainly singing from the same page; Mary would always tell it like it was.

"Being sincere is a rare quality these days Mary, that is what I like about you; you certainly don't beat around the bush." The game was now 20 minutes old and Lakeside was still losing 1-0. Two familiar faces could be seen on the touchline. It was Mr Nick Symonds and Mr Andrew Mann; they were both out walking when they bumped into each other. "What's going on here then?" said Nick to Andrew

"Some of the lads from our school are playing a friendly match against a mixture of lads from around the area, thought it might give me an opportunity to see what talent we may have missed, after all, we are still searching for more talent." With the focus now firmly on the match, it wasn't long before one of the Lakeland lads was brought down and got injured. You could see the concern on the face of all of his teammates. "How are you feeling Chris?" said Liam the team captain.

"Not too good Liam."

"You were well out of it for a few seconds Chris".

"Yes, I thought so. I felt I went out quicker than a broken light bulb. Chris did his best to get up, but only to fall back down again. "I can't stand up on my leg without it hurting, said Chris;" I don't think I can carry on".

"Ok, I will get you off then Chris; there is no point in making it worse."

"Toby, get yourself warmed up, you're on," shouted Liam across to the sidelines.

"What's going on Holly?" asked Mary. "It looks like someone is hurt, hope they are not badly injured; it looks like Chris Bedson, one of Toby's friends."

"Yes, seems like you're right Mary, and also it looks like Toby is coming onto the field of play."

"Come on Toby, show them how to play, woo woo woo," cried Mary. Back on the sideline, Nick and Andrew were making notes of what was going on. "Anyone caught your eye yet Nick?"

"Well, Liam Fenwick would be the obvious one, also the full-back Luke Farrell, strong as an Ox that one."

"Who's that coming onto the field now in place of Chris Bedson?"

"Not sure Andrew, hold on, it's that kid who came to the school trials two weeks ago, Toby Travis, He was awful, I think it's all downhill from here now Andrew."

"Well you don't need to look that shocked Nick, but yeah, I know what you mean."

"Toby, I want you to shore up the defence, we are getting overrun in that area," requested Liam. In the beginning, Toby was feeling a little bit out of his comfort zone but then started to play some good passes. Unfortunately, one of his passes went astray that landed right at the feet of George Bulldog who smashed it into the back of the net for 2-0. "Cheers for that Toby," said George sarcastically, "thank you for my early gift-wrapped birthday present."

"Well done George, great goal," could be heard from the rest of his teammates.

"Don't get involved with George's antics Toby; don't let it get to you," said Liam. Toby was now feeling miserable; his performance was going from bad to worse as the score increased to 3-0 just before half-time. Mary and Holly were trying to keep up the team's spirits by cheering them along.

"Come on Lakeside let's get one back," shouted Holly. Just then the whistle went to bring the first half to an end. You could see the despondency in the team as they trundled off the field with their heads on their chin straps.

"Not looking good is it Holly, without stating the obvious, I would say they are not very happy."

"You don't say, Mary, now I wonder what gives you that impression; maybe the fact that they are walking off looking down at their boots. They now have a ten-minute break before the second half starts; let's hope they have a better second half." Meanwhile, Nick and Andrew weren't holding back with their comments.

"Told you about that Travis boy Andrew; couldn't hit a barn door at a metre that one." "Are you planning on stopping for the second half Nick?"

"Well no, I wasn't planning on staying, that said, I've not got much else to do, so yes why not."

"Fancy a drink after the match down the Feathers Nick?"

"Yeah, now you're talking Andrew, why not, I could just drown a pint of lager." Back in the dressing room, Liam was getting stuck into to the team for the feeble effort that was being shown by his troops. A lot of what Liam had to say wasn't directly aimed at Toby; he knew that Toby would struggle against a very good team. With the half-time break almost over; Liam had a plan he wanted to put into action.

"Toby, I want you to play up front on the right wing, I want you to get as many crosses in as you can. I want you to attack their wing backs; I'll be waiting in the middle for the ball. William, I want you to follow Bulldog where ever he goes, take him out of the match. I want you to keep him in your pocket at all times. Let's use the space, let's pass the ball into the space for our players to run onto. Toby, how are you finding the boots that a borrowed you?"

"To be perfectly honest, not that good Liam, I guess I will just have to get used to them."

"Well, you do have a choice Toby. What about your boots, have you brought them with you?"

"Yes, they are in my bag, are you saying I should wear them."

"Only if you want to, let us just say if I was in your boots, I would give them a try. Go and put them on quickly, before the game kicks off." With Toby now struggling to get his boots laced up, the game was about to start. "Hurry up Toby," shouted his team players. Toby just made it onto the field at the amusement of his school teachers Mr Symonds and Mr Mann. "Can't even get on to the pitch in time for the second half, he would be late for his own funeral that one," said Nick.

"That's a little bit harsh Nick, but I know where you are coming from." Meanwhile, on the football pitch, Liam's plan was working a treat; and with only ten minutes gone, Toby got the ball in his own half. With George now being man marked by William McMullan, Toby ran up the wing like a greyhound. At first, you could see Toby cutting inside and then outside taking out two players in quick succession. The space now opened up in front of Toby allowing him to deliver the most perfect of crosses right onto the head of Liam Fenwick. Bang! Into the net it went. "Well done Toby," screamed Mary with delight.

"Great goal Liam, well done Toby," shouted Holly. Nick and Andrew were lost for words. "Wow! Where did that come from Andrew; was that Toby Travis who ran down the wing like a greyhound."

"I'm not sure Nick; it couldn't have been, could it?" Andrew needed some sort of clarification of what he thought he saw, so turned to a friend of Toby's who was watching the match by the sideline. "Was that Toby Travis who crossed the ball for Liam to head in?" asked Andrew.

"Yes," said Toby's friend, "great cross wasn't it?"

"Great cross, it was brilliant, I'm in shock! Where on earth did that come from?"

"Got me beat," said Nick who overheard the conversation. With Nick and Andrew now fully focused on the match, it had them thinking, "*Do we have a potential match-winner in our midst.*" The game was now ebbing and flowing with Lakeside having most of the possession. Toby played a wonderful one-two passing manoeuver with William, but instead of running down the wing like Liam instructed him to do, something mysterious happened. Toby's' boots came to life once more, as if they had a mind of their own. Toby could hear Liam shouting strenuously to cross the ball; however, Toby's' boots were having none of it. Toby took on three defenders and passed them with ease. With a fourth defender now imminent and looking to bring Toby to the ground, Toby let fly with a beautifully executed curling peach of a shot into the top right-hand corner of the net from 25 yards out. It brought so much excitement from all of his teammates who were jumping all over him; 3-2, and still ten minutes to go. "Did you see that Nick," said Andrew, an absolute blinder of a goal!"

"Yes, and there's still 10 minutes to go, plenty of time to press for an equaliser, come on Lakeside you can do it," yelled Nick. The performance from Toby was now getting everyone excited, even the opposition were stunned. Meanwhile, Mary and Holly were almost doing cartwheels, they had turned into cheerleaders. "Toby is playing really well Holly," said Mary, "I didn't realise he was that good."

"Neither did I Mary," feeling rather disorientated by Toby's performance. "I quite like the look of Liam Fenwick, not only can he play football, but I think he is a bit of a dish. I got talking to him at Toby's birthday party; he was such a laugh."

"Oh yes, so maybe I should be asking you some personal questions. Would you sleep with him, Holly?"

"Wild horses wouldn't stop me, Mary."

"Not one for beating around the bush then Holly; tell it as it is why don't you."

It was now entering the final embers of the match. Lakeside school had now got the bit between their teeth; pressing hard for an equaliser that unfortunately was not forthcoming. With a slight break in play, Toby was called over by Liam for a last-minute tactical talk. "Toby, I want you to drag all of their defence over to the right-hand side of the pitch, the way you are playing I can guarantee you that their defence will follow you. Then, with a bit of luck, it will leave enough space for William and me to penetrate their full-backs."

"Ok Liam," said Toby. On the sidelines, Nick and Andrew were wondering why Toby was isolating himself from the rest of the team. "Don't know what's going on there," said Nick, "surely they would be better with Toby down the middle; he's doing nothing out there." Toby made his way over to the touchline, and as guessed by Liam, two defenders followed him. The centre area of the pitch was now looking sparse, giving Liam and William the space they required to get a shot on goal. As the ball was pumped up field by Lakeside it landed at the feet of William. William turned swiftly and spotted Liam running at speed into the penalty area. All that was needed now was an accurate pass to Liam and he would be in on goal. A sublime pass was what William delivered. Liam was now in on goal; a great shot that seemed all over the equaliser was miraculously saved by the goalkeeper, only for the rebound to fall to William who slammed the ball home; 3-3, who would have believed it? Even the school teachers were jumping up and down on the sideline, maybe because they would now be venturing into the land of Milk and Honey.

Toby had no idea that his PT teachers Mr Symonds and Mr Mann were watching the game as the final whistle blew for full-time in a hard-fought game. All eyes were now on Toby and the Lakeside Secondary School football team as they made their way into the changing room; they would the topic of conversation when the team returned to school on Monday morning. Meanwhile, Mr Symonds and Mr Mann would have some thinking to do. There would be questions to answer, why did Toby play so well? Why didn't he show that sort of ability at the school trials? Should he now be considered for the school football team? Even Toby couldn't make any sense of it; talking to his father at some point might provide Toby with all the answers.

CHAPTER 4

TOBY NEEDS SOME ANSWERS

Monday morning arrived quicker than Toby would have liked; his paper round and his first day back to school is not the most desirable things to wake-up to. Already in the shop was Mary's mum. "Well done Toby," she said, Mary has told me all about the game on Saturday, did you enjoy it?"

"Thank you Mrs Callaghan, yes it was enjoyable,"

"Does that mean you will get into the school football team then Toby?"

"Probably not, it was just a friendly game, it dint really have any bearing on the school football team. The P.T teachers have to see you play, that's how they make their decision.

"Well maybe some of the lads you were playing with might put a good word in for you."

"I doubt it Mrs Callaghan, we will just have to wait and see. Back at home Toby's mum was getting breakfast ready just as Toby came walking through the door. "Right on queue Toby, said his mum; I'm just finishing off your breakfast, get yourself sat down. "Are you walking with Mary today?"

"Yes, in about 20 minutes all being well." All of a sudden, a cry from the other end of the kitchen could be heard. "Mum, have you seen my school bag?" asked Holly who was now getting ready for school.

"Yes, it's on the floor in the hallway, right next to Toby's football bag."

"Thanks mum."

"Toby, I will take your school bag to the Laundrette and get your football shirt washed, you can take it back to school tomorrow."

"Ok mum, thanks for that; I will tell Mr Symonds if he asks me where it is." Toby arrived back at school to find that is performance had not gone unnoticed. All Toby could hear around the playground was, "that's the kid over there, the one that everyone is talking about, apparently he played a right blinder." Toby wasn't one for wanting to be in the limelight, fair to say; it was something that Toby would have to get use to in the coming days. At the Lilly Pink girls' school, Mary was also the talk of the school, after all, she was Toby's girlfriend. Her best friend Lucy though, wanted to know all about the night Mary stayed over at Toby's house. "Come on then Mary," said Lucy; "spill the beans, I want to know everything that went on behind closed doors last night?" Mary paused for a moment, believing that Lucy might know about Toby's father coming back as a spiritual Ghost.

"I take it you are referring to Toby, aren't you?"

"Well yes of course, who else, unless there was someone else in the room." '*If only she knew the truth*', Mary was thinking.

"It was a lovely evening, and yes, Toby and I actually lay under the quilt together; only for about 5 minutes though, and yes, we both had pyjamas on before you ask."

"So cool Mary, so you didn't, you know, don't make me spell it out Mary, you know what I mean."

"No! We certainly did not. I have told you everything now Lucy, so let's leave it at that," said Mary in a bright and breezy way. Down at the Laundrette Toby's mum arrived for work, along with Toby's football bag. "Morning Hilda, Morning Marge," said Rose.

"Morning Rose," replied Hilda and Marge."

"What's in the bag Rose," said Hilda.

"It's Nothing to concern you about; it just a ferret."

"A ferret!" said Hilda. "Is it dead?"

"It will be in a minute when I put it in the wash; I can't stand the smell of the retched thing." Hilda was now looking horrified at the thought of seeing a ferret being spun around in the window of the washing machine. "You can't put it in the washing machine Rose just because it smells."

"Well if you hang around long enough Hilda, you will be able to see for yourself. I can't believe that you are so gullible Hilda, as if you would believe that I would put a ferret n the washing machine, I wouldn't even dream of it."

"You had me going there for a minute Rose; I think I need a sit down with a hot brew after that. I am now just wondering whether to ask you the same question again."

"Fire away Hilda."

"Ok Rose, what have you in the bag if you don't mind me asking?"

"Toby's football kit, he was playing at the weekend so needs to take his football shirt back to school tomorrow,"

"Did they win?" asked Marge getting in on the conversation.

"Not too sure to be totally honest, think they might have drawn." Rose started taking Toby's football kit out of his bag before coming across Toby's dishevelled football boots, the ones from his father. "Holy smoke, it must have been muddy on Saturday; look at the state of his boots; covered in mud. I'll put them out in the back yard and clean them later," said Rose. Back at Lakeside Secondary School, Toby was approached by Liam. "Toby, I've just been chatting to Mr Symonds, he wants you to report to the gym on his lunch-break."

"Why, what in heaven have I done wrong now?"

"Well, unless you have been harassing the lollipop lady outside the school gates, my guess would be it has something to do with your performance on Saturday."

"How would they know about my performance on Saturday, did you say something?"

"No, I never said a word Toby, maybe someone else told them about how you played."

"Yeah, you never know, anyway, thanks for passing on the message Liam, I will go and see him and let you know what they wanted me for." It was now lunch time and Toby could be seen making his way into the gym. "Toby Travis, just the man" said Mr Symonds, "take a seat in my office, be with you in a second." Toby took a seat and waited with bated breath for Mr Symonds to arrive. Seconds later, Mr Symonds and Mr Mann entered the room where Toby was sitting looking very professional. "Ok Toby, I suppose you are wondering what I want to talk to you about," said Mr Symonds.

"Well yes, I did wonder, it certainly did have me feeling a little concerned. It's nothing to do with the lollipop lady outside the school gates, is it?

"Not sure I'm with you on that one Toby?"

"It's just that someone mentioned that I have been harassing her, oh and by the way it's not true. Why would I want to do that?

"I have no idea Toby; now can we get on to the real reason why I wanted to see you."

"Yes, sorry for digressing."

"No problem Toby. Well you unquestionably don't need to feel concerned any more Toby. Did you know that Mr Mann and I saw you playing football on Saturday?"

"Really, no sir, I had no idea. Where were you hiding?"

"We weren't hiding anywhere Toby; it wasn't a planned reunion. I was just taking a walk; you know trying to charm the birds out of the trees and inhaling some fresh air. It was then I noticed there was a game of football going on; Mr Mann was also was doing exactly the same thing."

"What, you were also charming birds out of the trees Mr Mann?"

"No Toby, I certainly was not there to charm the birds out of the trees. I was getting some fresh air."

"Anyway Toby," said Mr Symonds. We noticed that a lot of the lads from Lakeside School were playing, so decided to stay for a while to see if we could spot some more talent for the school team. So now does it make in any clearer why we would like to talk to you then?"

"Well I suppose I did have a good second half, is that what you are referring to?"

"Yes, that is exactly what we are referring to Toby. Andrew, he says I suppose I did half a good second half. A good second half! You had a sensationally second half Toby, I owe you an apology. After the school trials, and by the way, thank you for turning up to the trials, myself and Mr Mann, were really slating you off, we categorically didn't see anything at all of any value in your football to suggest to us that you were anywhere near good enough to make the school football team, in fact, we saw absolutely nothing at all that was telling us you could even play football, it was diabolical, it goes to show how wrong we were; even a stopped clock is correct twice a day Where did that display come from on Saturday?"

"Well first of all, thank you for being so brutally honest with me, but I think what you said was little over the top. You will have to excuse me if I don't laugh at your remarks; however, I guess I can see where you are coming from."

"So where did that display come from Toby?"

"I'm not sure sir," said Toby trying not to give anything away about his magical boots.

"Well Toby, Mr Mann and I would like to see more of your skills, and if you continue to perform like you did on Saturday, we will have no hesitations in putting you into the school football team."

"Wow! That would be amazing if that was to happen sir."

"Well if you earn the right then you earn your stripes, that's how it works Toby; If you can show us that type of display again then you will for definite be in the school football team. We would like you to come and train with the school team this Wednesday after school, is that ok."

"That would be fine sir," smiled Toby. Toby couldn't wait to tell Liam and the rest of the team about his good news. A few minutes later Toby caught up with Liam. "Liam over here now, I have some exciting news to tell you."

"What's that then Toby?"

"I have been invited to join the school football team, just like you said Liam.

"That is brilliant news Toby, knew you could make it."

"Well I wasn't too sure, thanks for having faith in me Liam."

"Mr Symonds and Mr Mann have invited me to the training session on Wednesday after school."

"Fantastic Toby, I really look forward to training with you on Wednesday; oh, and by the way, make sure you don't forget your football boots Toby."

"Of course I won't, anyway catch you later." Toby was now feeling reluctant to tell anyone else about his good news in-case it all blew up in his face; the fewer people he told then the fewer people he would have to disappoint if he didn't make the school football team. Shortly after arriving home, Toby saw Mary loitering with intent in front of her house, looking like she was hoping to catch Toby as he came home. "Hi Toby, what sort of day have you had today?"

"It's been quite a normal day with nothing really exciting happening; as the saying goes, 'nothing really to write home about' Mary."

"Do you fancy a catch-up later, I could come around after tea if you like, or you could come to my house for tea, sure my mum will be fine with that."

"I think my mum has already got plans for tea, and not only that, I have got things to be getting on with tonight Mary, maybe another night."

"Oh, ok Toby, it was just a suggestion, I will just have to stay in and wash my hair." Mary was feeling very despondent now; she just wasn't use to Toby saying no to her advances. "I will catch you tomorrow morning Mary."

"Ok Toby, see you tomorrow." Toby was burning up inside lying to Mary; he could see the look on Mary's face when he declined her invitation. A relationship should be made on trust and not deceit. This change in Toby's life was something that he was finding difficult to deal with; I mean to say, you are

14 years old and falling in love with your next-door neighbour, your father who you have never seen, visits you as a spiritual Ghost, and now you have a pair of football WW1 football boots that have a mind of their own. It was far too much for Toby to deal with.

Mean while, Mary needs someone to talk to; she decides to give Lucy a call for some advice from her mobile phone. Lying on her bed Lucy sees' Mary's name come up on her mobile phone. "Hi Mary, how's things with you?"

"Well, it's nice to hear someone is feeling happy, that's actually why I phoned you Lucy."

"Toby seems a little off at the moment; I can't quite put my finger on it. I just made a suggestion about meeting up later, believing that he would have jumped at the opportunity, well to cut to the chase, he just said he had other things he needed to be getting on with; I wasn't expecting that."

"Then don't ask questions if you are not fully prepared for the answer."

"Some fat help you are Lucy, what book did you get that from?"

"I'm sorry Mary, it wasn't meant to come across like that, what I'm trying to say is, don't investigate in to it to deeply, Toby may be telling you the truth Mary, I'm sure he would have jumped at the chance if it was possible. From what I can see, Toby loves you, just give him a little space; that would be my advice."

"Yeah, I will ask him if he would like to go the park on Saturday, he can stand at one end of the park and I will stand at the other. Do you think that would be enough space?"

"Don't be so dramatic Mary; you are acting like a child now."

"Yeah you're right Lucy, sorry about that, I just feel angry. What you said makes a lot of sense. I think that's what I will do. Anyway, he did say he would see me in the morning as usual, so it isn't all bad."

"Well there you go then Mary, see what he has to say tomorrow, but remember, don't go pushing it too far, let Toby talk and you listen, that's my advice"

"Didn't see you around school today Lucy, were you hiding from me?"

I wish, only joking Mary, I had a lot of school work to catch up on."

"How was your weekend Lucy?"

"Pretty boring if I'm being perfectly honest Mary, I need to get a boyfriend, what about you?"

"I've got a boyfriend, don't need another one."

"Now you are winding me up Mary, you know I dint mean that, I meant how was your weekend?"

Yes, it was a really good weekend seeing as you ask. I went to see Toby play football really enjoyed it, then on Sunday Toby and I went to KFC."

"So pleased for you and Toby Mary, may it continue."

"Who's that shouting Lucy?

"On my way mum, it's my mum Mary shouting from the foot of the stairs, not sure what she wants. Anyway, I better go and see before she throws a tantrum."

"Thanks Lucy, catch you tomorrow, take care." Later on that evening, Toby is sitting on his bed hoping to get in touch with his father. At least an hour had gone by without any sign at all that Toby's father was going to grace Toby with his presence. Toby now had to think of a way to get in touch with the other side, the land of the living dead. With the lights off and the room completely in the dark, Toby decided to call his father. "Dad, dad, are you there dad, if you are, please make yourself known to me. I've lots of unanswered questions that need answering dad," said Toby to the point of begging. "Why are you not answering me dad," said Toby scanning his head around the room, looking for any signs of his father's presence.

Toby was now becoming more and more agitated. "You only show yourself when it suites you, why don't you show yourself when I want to talk to you. Toby was now at the point of giving up on ever talking to his father again. Just then, Toby noticed the photo frame of his father starting to move, very gently at first and then, just before it flung itself to the floor, Toby was there ready to catch it. A ghostly figure started to appear, just like the other two times Toby spoke to his dad. Toby was now feeling a sense of relief, his father was about to show himself once more. "Toby, how are you?" said his father.

"I feel overwhelmingly better now dad, I thought you had gone walk about, I was tempted to send out a search party to fine you. I have loads of questions I need to ask you."

"As I said Toby, I am always looking out for you. You caught me at a bad time; I was watching a really good zombie movie."

"A zombie movie dad, pull the other leg."

"Now that's not a nice thing to say Toby, you know I can't pull anything. I can move things with my mind, but that's as far as it goes.

"Ok then, well if you can see me, why don't you help me when I need you?"

"It depends what you mean by help."

"Well, I would like you to take control of my emotions so I don't get into trouble."

"It doesn't work like that Toby, I can give you encouragement, I can give you guidance, I can even give you advice, but I can't change freewill. There are lots of decisions that you will have to make for yourself; in fact, I have less control over you now than if I was alive."

"Freewill, what do you mean by freewill dad?"

"It means that I have no power to change the way you do things, I have no power in what you want to do in your life; for instance, I can't stop you seeing Mary, that as to be your choice Toby."

"So are you saying you don't want me to see Mary anymore?"

"No Toby, that is exactly what I am not saying, I like Mary, but the decision to have Mary as your girlfriend would have to be yours, does that make any sense to you Toby."

"So if I wanted to marry Mary, you couldn't stop me, is that what you are saying dad?"

"You've got it Toby, but I hope you are a long way from getting married. Anyway, what is it you wanted to ask me Toby?"

"I would like to ask you more about these so-called magical football boots. I played a game on Saturday and at first, I played with my friend's boots; rubbish is a word I would describe my performance, I couldn't have hit a barn door at two metres."

"Well I'm sure you weren't that bad Toby. So then what happened next?"

"I decided to wear your football boots dad, just like you said. I thought I would give them a try; I was just hoping that no one would notice how much out of date they were, I just couldn't take anymore embarrassment."

"Well I was watching Toby, from the sidelines, didn't you see me? I'm only joking Toby; I am invisible to everyone; even you when I want to be. I can control who sees me Toby, that's why I let Mary see me the other night."

"Well then you would have seen how well I played after that, I couldn't do anything wrong, the boots were playing the game for me, it was incredible. So are they really magical dad, or is there something else I need to know?"

"Yes Toby, they are magical, and there is nothing else you need to know apart from they will only play from you. If they were to come in to the hands of someone else, they would have the adverse affect, whoever came in possession of the boots would find it difficult to even kick the ball in a straight line. Keep them safe Toby and they will serve you well, if you decide at any time not to wear them, then you may struggle."

"I am finding it difficult to keep the knowledge of the boots a secret dad, and also the fact that I am talking to you. I know my friends will think I have lost my marbles; there is just no way that I could ever convince them that my dad is a ghost and that I speak to him."

"Then don't tell them, people only believe something if they can see it Toby; if they can't see me, and that would be my choice, then there isn't a problem, it doesn't matter if they don't believe you. As far as the boots are concerned, well trying to get someone to believe that your boots are magical would be like getting someone to believe that the moon is made out of cheese and you have had piece." That similarity of that remark made Toby laugh out loudly, but also had him understanding what his father meant. Toby was a lot wiser now after talking to his father, but still needed to keep quiet until he felt the time was right to tell his mum and sister. It was now morning and Toby could be seen with Mary walking to the bus stop.

"Not wanting to pry, but did you have a nice evening-in last night Toby?

"Yes, and you are not prying Mary. I'm sorry I was a bit off last night, just had a lot of thinking to do."

"And what about now?" are you feeling better now Toby?"

"Well let's just say things are a lot clearer. I was actually talking to my father again last night, he says he likes you, likes you a lot Mary."

"Oh, well that's nice Toby, nice to have your father's approval. What else did he have to say?"

"Well first of all Mary, everything I tell you must not go any further than you and I, please promise me that."

"I like having secrets Toby, so I have no problem with that. A woman's heart is an ocean of secrets; you would do well to remember that." Toby explained everything to Mary about what his father had spoken about; and in particular the magic in the boots. Mary found the story about the boots intriguing but hard to believe, so when Toby explained to her about his well above average performance on Saturday, she did extremely well to hide her feelings about what she believed was poppy-cock. "Oh by the way Mary, the effort I put in on Saturday and the level I played at didn't go unnoticed." Mr Symonds and Mr Mann were watching from the side lines, they had a chat with me yesterday and want me to train with the school team tomorrow night."

"Wow! That's great news isn't it Toby?"

"I presume so, not sure if I really deserve it though, it's the boots that make me play well."

"Just think of it as a gift Toby, a gift from haven. People are gifted in different ways," some are gifted with a beautiful voice; some are gifted musicians, just except the gift Toby."

"Yeah, and some have got the gift of the gab Mary."

"Toby Travis, I don't know what you mean, so glad to see that you've got your sense of humour back," chuckled Mary.

With that said, Toby gave Mary a firm hug, a hug that had Mary feeling so much better again. One more day and Toby would have the chance to show off his skills, what would be the chance of Toby messing it up again, surly not.

CHAPTER 5

LITTLE WHITE LIES

Wednesday morning arrived. The weather was inclement, in other words, raining cats and dogs. Suddenly there was a knock on the front door; it was Mary holding an umbrella.

"Hi Toby, my mum asked me to ask you whether you would like a lift this morning, and she will also pick you up later."

"That would be great Mary, how thoughtful of your mum; would my sister be able to get a lift too?"

"Yes sorry, I meant to say your sister would be more than welcome."

"Just come in a moment Mary out of the rain."

"Mum," shouted Toby, "Mary's mum said Holly I can get a lift with her mum today, and she will also pick us up later after school is finished."

"That's nice of her, save you getting a good soaking." Hold on a minute, haven't you got football training after school, Toby?"

"Oh damn, I'd forgotten about that mum, not sure whether that will work."

"Of course, it will work Toby, give me a call when you're ready, and I will come and pick you up."

"Ok, cheers for that mum, then that's that settled." With Toby and Holly now on their way to school, the Travis household was feeling empty. Toby's mum decided to check on Bob and Brenda at No 43.

"Hi Bob," said Rose as the door opened.

"Oh, come on in Rose out of the rain, not fit for dogs this weather."

"Brenda, it's Rose," yelled Bob.

"Just wondering if you've got any laundry you would like cleaning at the laundrette," I'm on my way now; I will have it back to you by lunchtime."

"Thank you, Rose," said Brenda, "so nice to have neighbours that are always willing to help out."

"Nonsense, don't be silly Brenda, it's nice to have neighbours who are so undisruptive, couldn't have wished for better neighbours."

"Thank you, Rose; so nice of you to say so. Well, I do have a few bed sheets that need cleaning if you don't mind taking them."

"Of course not Brenda, give them here, I'll put them in the back of the car." Rose made her way to the laundrette. On arrival, it was the normal gossip and cuppa with Hilda and Marge before getting stuck into work." Such a filthy day today Rose," said Hilda, "not even fit for cats to be out on the streets."

"How's your family Rose?" asked Marge sipping her hot cup of tea.

"Well do you mean apart from Holly always being secretive, Toby's in love with Mary, Bob and Brenda acting as if they are part of the home guard, and the weather is awful, I would say yes, everything is fine Marge."

"Oh, that's good then, sounds like everything is under control." After their 15-minute tea break and chewing each other's ears off, Rose got stuck into getting Bob and Brenda's sheets cleaned before the laundrette got too busy. It was now launch time; time for Rose to head home.

"Don't forget the sheets Rose," shouted Hilda, we can't have Bob and Brenda sleeping on a naked mattress."

"I'm pretty sure they will have more than one set of sheets Hilda. But no, I haven't forgotten them; I've already got them in my car Hilda, but thanks for reminding me anyway."

Back home, Rose took the bed sheets out of her car and gave them to Brenda. "Thank you so much, Rose, they smell so fresh." How much do I owe you?"

"Owe me, don't be silly Brenda; you owe me nothing, glad to be of service. I'm just so glad that the rain has stopped now Brenda."

"Yes, same here, I have a water feature in my garden that wasn't there this morning. Have you got time for a brew Rose?"

"I better not, but thank you anyway, got my housework to do: ironing, polishing, you know the usual things, it won't do on its own even though the kids think it will."

"I know exactly what you mean Rose, my two were the same when they were growing up, in a nice way, I'm so glad they have now grown up and making their own way in life. I love seeing the grandchildren knowing that I can hand them back at the end of the day."

"So true Brenda," replied Rose chuckling out loud. "Anyway, must be off, I will catch you later; bye for now Bob, take care." It was now 3.30; Rose was getting stuck into her ironing when she got a call on her mobile. "Hi, Rose, it's Hilda here from the laundrette,"

"What can I do for you, Hilda?"

"Well, I was just putting out the rubbish before locking up and come across an old pair of football boots by the back door."

"Football boots!" replied Rose feeling lost in the conversation. "Don't know if I can help you there Hilda."

"Not an issue, maybe someone has just binned them, I will stick them in the skip, they look like they belong there anyway."

"Ok catch you later Hilda, sorry I can't help you, thanks for phoning." As Rose hung up, the boots were already finding their way into the skip. Seconds later with Rose now remembering that she would have to pick Toby up later from school, the penny dropped. "*Oh my giddy aunt, they must be Toby's, I must have forgotten to bring them back from the laundrette on Monday.*" Rose was now in a state of panic and desperate to call Hilda back before she locks up for the night.

"*Pick up Hilda*" said Rose to herself; *"pick up the phone."* Just then Hilda answered. "Hi Rose, you ok? You sound panicky."

"No, I'm not ok, and yes I am panicking. Where are you now Hilda?"

"Just about to drive away, why what's the problem?"

"The boots, that's the problem. Don't you drive anywhere Hilda, what did you do with the boots?"

"The boots, oh don't worry Rose, I have put them in the skip."

"In the skip, they are Toby's boots; I'd forgotten that I had left them outside on Monday because they were filthy dirty."

"Well they're even dirtier now Rose, I would say they look more like two drowned rats. I will tell you what though Rose, you are actually lucky they are still here."

"What do you mean Hilda? lucky that they are still there."

"Well Monday is the day when the bins get emptied; it seems like even the bin men didn't want them."

"That's not fair or funny Hilda, you don't really mean that."

"Probably not, but you must admit it was a bit funny, I could even hear you sniggering under your breath Rose."

"Well, maybe I did find it a bit funny. Look, just stay where you are Hilda, I'm on my way now as I speak. Toby is going to need them in half an hour; he has got school football training."

"Ok, see you soon Rose, drive carefully." Meanwhile, at Lakeside Secondary School, Toby had absolutely no idea that his boots weren't in his football bag as he made his way to the Gym to get changed. "Looking forward to training tonight Toby?" asked Liam.

"Yes," said Toby, "I actually am for a change." It was only then when Toby was getting changed that he realised his boots were missing. "Anybody seen my boots," said Toby, thinking, *someone may be playing a prank on him.* "Not me," was the reply from all of the lads.

"Well someone must have seen them, they can't have just got up and walked away, can they?" With a look of desperation written all over his face, Toby was now feeling concerned. Toby continued searching in the hope that he would find them somewhere in the changing room but to no avail. "You can borrow my spare pair, Toby," said Liam, "I have brought them with me."

"No, I need my boots Liam; I can play so much better in my boots."

"It's only a training session Toby, not a real game; I think you proved yourself on Saturday that you are good enough for the school team, that's why you are here tonight. We all have the occasional off day Toby, so stop worrying and get these boots on." Back at the laundrette, Rose was just arriving with 'chew my dirt and smell my rubber' written all over her face. "Here you are Rose," said Hilda passing her Toby's football boots. "On your way now Rose, go on, get going quickly before it's too late" Back at the school, the lads were warming up on the field. "On my head Toby," said Liam, "just like on Saturday.' Toby was a little off the mark, and Liam would have needed to be as tall as a Giraffe to have reached it.

Toby was gutted and knew there was worse to come. Luckily for Toby, it was just the warm-up session that meant most of what he did went unnoticed. "Ok lads, get lined up behind the goal in a straight line," said Mr Symonds with Mr Mann by his side. "Let's get you lot working those muscles. I want ten minutes of hard graft before we start practising some tactics. After that, I will then split you up into two teams for a ten-minute each half game."

After the ten-minute fitness session, the lads were given a 5-minute break while Mr Symonds and Mr Mann explained certain formations and styles of play; the way they were breathing meant it was probably a good job they were given a break. About halfway through the speech, there was what seemed like a rude disruption. "Toby, Toby, over here darling, I've got your boots."

"Are we expecting any visitors Nick?"

"Not to my knowledge Andrew.

"Can I help you madam?" said Andrew looking bemused.

"Yes, I have brought Toby Travis's football boots; he accidentally left them at home."

"Oh really, just put them down on the grass, I will make sure he gets them."

"Thank you," said Rose waving frantically at Toby. "How long do you think they will be?"

"I would estimate around half an hour if it all goes well."

"Well, there will be no point in me going home then, is it ok if I stay and watch."

"Yes, that's fine Mrs Travis."

"Oh Rose is fine," she said with a flirtatious smile.

"Well my name is Andrew, Andrew Mann, and yes there is not a day that goes past without someone reminding me of my name. Fortunately, all the boys have to address me as Mr Mann or Sir."

"Not sure I follow Andrew."

"Andy is short for Andrew, which translates into Andy Mann, does it make sense now Rose."

"Yes it does, I understand perfectly now," said Rose smirking.

"It could be worse though," said Andrew. "

"How could it be worse," said Rose looking puzzled.

"Well, I have a friend that teaches at another school not too far from here, his name is Mr Pipe, Mr Dwayne Pipe." It took Rose a second or two before putting the two names together, "Dwayne Pipe." This had Rose in fits of laughter, so much that it caused Mr Symonds to look around. "Is everything ok Andrew?" said Nick curiously."

"Yes, no problem Nick, Mrs Travis has just brought Toby's football boots that he accidentally left at home."

"Oh, ok then." Andrew and Rose just gave each other a huge smile like it was their little secret. I think it made them both feel young again. "Ok Toby, get your boots on, and then I will split you up into two teams of equal quality," said Mr Symonds. Mr Symonds and Mr Mann were watching carefully to see who was shining, oh, and Toby's mum. Toby was put on the right wing to start with, and he certainly did not disappoint; his boots were on form once more. A long ball forward to Toby saw him pull the ball down and then swivel almost in the same movement, leaving the defender in his wake. Toby then cut inside another defender before firing home in the right-hand bottom corner; Toby couldn't have had a more positive start.

"Wow, was that my Toby who scored, Andrew?"

"Yes it was, that was some goal Rose; Toby has come on leaps and bounds over the last two weeks."

"Maybe it has something to do with his boots."

"What do you mean by that Rose?"

"Oh nothing Andrew, said Rose nearly letting the cat out of the bag. "He just said he plays better in the boots that were handed down to him from his late father."

"Oh well, whatever it is it seems to be working."

By half-time, it was 2-0 so Mr Symonds decided to swap some of the players around.

"Toby, I want to see what you are like on the left-hand side, swap with William McMullan. William, I want you to play left back and where possible feed the ball down the wing to Toby." The tactics worked a treat, William's side-rule pass sent Toby flying down the wing, and within seconds the ball was in the net. Toby sent the most perfect ball across for Liam to smash home. Mr Symonds and Mr Mann had seen all they needed to see for this session; it has been a long time since Lakeside Secondary School had a team that was capable of winning the four counties cup; a cup that is played for by all the high schools in the county.

"Ok lads, get yourselves changed and get yourself back home, I will see you tomorrow," said Mr Symonds.

"Oh Andrew, thank you for letting me watch the game," said Rose, "I really enjoyed it."

"Anytime Rose. Maybe I'll catch you around." That evening it was Mary's turn to be invited to Toby's house for tea. Whilst sitting around the table, the topic of conversation was varying from Toby's football to the approach of Holly's exams. "Do you believe in Ghosts Mum?" said Toby inquisitively, "you know, spirits and things."

"I'm not sure Toby, what a strange question, why do you ask?"

"Oh, it was just a book I was reading in the school Library today,"

"Why were you drawn to a book on Ghosts Toby?" said Holly curiously.

"I saw a programme on TV last week and was taken in by it." You could see Mary glancing over to Toby that was closely observed by Holly. Holly could tell that Toby was telling a little white lie so continued with her questioning.

"What programme was that then Toby, I wouldn't mind watching it." Toby knew he was in trouble now with his unprepared answers and that Holly was seeing through him like a crystal ball. Because of Holly's investigation-type questions, like she was trying to solve a murder; Toby was quick to change the subject.

"I can't remember Holly, you know me, I can't remember from one day to another. Anyway, thank you for bringing my boots today mum, I really don't know how they ended up not being in my bag."

"I've no idea Toby; I found them just outside the back door, you must have left them there on Saturday after your football game."

"A good job you did, hey mum."

"Yes it is Toby; it's a good job I remember things or we would be in a right mess."

"I was chatting to one of your football coaches today Toby, Mr Mann."

"Oh you mean Andy Mann."

"Yes Toby, Andrew Mann," said Toby's mum chuckling to herself.

"Andy Mann," said Mary. Mary and Holly couldn't hide their laughter, it didn't take Mary and Holly long to work out the funny side to Andrew's name.

"Sorry Mum," said Holly, "I didn't mean to laugh."

"Sorry Mrs Travis," said Mary.

"To be totally honest, if that was my name, I think I would get it changed straight away," said Rose. "Anyway Toby, back to your original question, I am slightly sceptical about spirits, you know, the other side and things. But I would say yes, I do believe in Ghosts. I just hope one day I will be able to talk to your father again. I very often have these moments when I am on my own and yes, I just feel that he is in the room with me, watching over me; probably just my imagination." Later on, that evening, with Toby in his bedroom, there was a gentle knock on Toby's door. "Are you a wake Toby?"

"Yes, come in Holly."

"Can we have a brotherly sisterly talk, Toby," said Holly with a serious look on her face.

"Yes of cause Holly, what about?"

"I think you know what it's about Toby. These last few nights I have heard voices coming from your room when I know there was no one in your room; Who were you talking to Toby? And tonight, while we were having tea, what was all this talking about Ghosts about? I could tell you were lying; would you mind telling me what's going on Toby?" Toby's little white lies were now catching up with him; how much longer can Toby keep the truth from Holly and his mum?

"Just give me a little longer Holly, and then I will tell you everything you want to know. Just trust me on this one Holly."

"Well, you better Toby; otherwise, I will say something to Mum."

CHAPTER 6

TOBY IS LEFT WITH NO CHOICE

By the following day, Toby had still managed to keep the lid on his father's presence, but it wasn't to last. Holly would not be deceived for much longer, she said to Toby that if he still continued being uncooperative by the end of the day, then she will tell mum that Mary was planning to sleep with him given the opportunity. On the way to school, Toby started explaining to Mary about what Holly had said. "I can't believe that Holly would do such an evil thing," said Mary.

"She's not evil Mary, she's just a cow.'

"Toby, that's not a nice thing to say about your sister, you can't go around saying things like that even if she is."

"I'm only joking Mary; she is not a cow, or any other farmland animal come to that. Mary always means well; we look out for each other all the time. Maybe it would be better to tell her the truth; keeping secrets from each other is not something we do."

"Ok Toby, so when do you plan on telling her?"

"Tonight, I will tell her tonight after tea, would you mind coming round to my house Mary, I think I would feel better if you were there with me, after all, you have seen my father as well."

"Yes of course I will Toby if it makes you feel better; two heads are better than one."

"What do you mean Mary, so Holly can smash our heads together?"

"No, you daft thing, well I hope she won't."

"I will send Holly a text now to let her know that I will talk to her when I get home after school." At school, Toby was told he was in the school football team for a game on Friday evening after school, along with Liam Fenwick, Chris Bedson, William McMullan and Mat White. Toby also noticed that George Bulldog was on the team; maybe this would be an opportunity to strike up a friendship with George. It was to be the final league game of the season against Darcy High School in Chester, a chance to win the league. A win would see Lakeside Secondary School finish top of the tree depending on other results. Although Toby was feeling excited, he had more concerning matters to deal with before Friday's game. As Toby arrived home from school, he was approached by the curtain twitchers, Bob and Brenda. "Hello Toby, would you mind doing me a favour," asked Brenda politely."

"Yes of course, what is it that you would like me to do Mrs Wilkinson?"

"Would you mind running an errand for me, Toby? I need some milk, I seem to have run out."

"Yes, I would gladly run an errand for you Mrs Wilkinson. I may as well go now before getting changed out of my school clothes." Brenda handed over a five-pound note to Toby and told him to get himself some sweets for his troubles.

"Thank you so much Mrs Wilkinson, that is very kind of you, I'll get on my way right now." Ten minutes later Toby arrived at the corner shop.

"Hello Mrs Callaghan," said Toby as he entered the shop, "just need some milk for Mrs Wilkinson. Is it ok for Mary to come around this evening after tea?"

"Yes, absolutely fine Toby; just don't keep her too long, it's a school day tomorrow."

"Well, I was thinking around 10-ish, would that be ok? There are quite a lot of things we need to go through, school work and things of that sort of nature.

"Well, that's a little late Toby, but yes ok then, I will make sure she has got her front door key with her."

"I'll take a bar of chocolate as well please Mrs Callaghan."

"Here you go Toby, be careful on the way home."

"Will do, bye Mrs Callaghan, catch you later." As Toby arrived home, his mum asked where he had been on his bike. Toby explained he had run an errand for Mrs Wilkinson, an errand that had Rose feeling proud of her son.

"Is Holly home mum?" asked Toby.

"Yes, she's in her bedroom; she arrived home about 20 minutes ago, why do you ask?"

"Oh no reason Mum, just something I need to talk to her about." Toby made his way upstairs to Holly's bedroom which was partly open. "Can I come in Holly," asked Toby with a little tap on the door

"Yes, I'm decent Toby, come in and close the door behind you."

"Sorry, I'm a little late, just been running an errand for Mrs Wilkinson."

"And here's me thinking you had run off with Mary, silly me, whatever gives me these ideas?"

"I've no idea Holly where you get these crazy ideas from; certainly not me. Anyway, on that note, Mary is coming around after tea this evening if that's ok with you?"

"Well, it depends on what she is coming for. Why does Mary have to come? I thought it was supposed to be a sort of secretive chat just between us two."

"Well yes it was, but you'll find out the reason later why I invited Mary, believe me, it is important that she comes."

"Well, it better be a good reason, Toby."

"Oh, it is definitely without doubt a good reason Holly, just wait until this evening and all will be revealed." Three hours later Mary arrived. "Come in Mary," said Mrs Travis, "Toby's expecting you." Mary was looking a little bit too provocative for Rose's liking: short denim skirt, low neck top along with make-up causing Rose to feel concerned. "Toby's upstairs in his bedroom with Holly I think, just go up."

"Thank you Mrs Travis." Mary galloped up the stairs like there was no tomorrow causing Toby and Holly to be startled by the noise.

"Don't take this the wrong way Mary, but I thought there was an Elephant loose in the house," said Toby."

"I'll forgive you this time Toby; I suppose I did make a bit of a noise."

"Anyway, come in Mary, and close the door behind you, we have got a lot of explaining to do, oh and by the way, love your short denim skirt."

"We will have less of that Toby," said Holly raising her eyebrows. Toby Mary and now Holly were gathered together in Toby's bedroom. With the lack of room, Toby suggested that they sit with their legs crossed on the carpet facing each other like they were going to tell a Ghost story. With the door closed and Toby's bedside light providing a glimmer of light, the scene was set.

"Ok Holly, about two weeks ago on my birthday, do you remember that Mum and I went into the attic."

"Yes, answered Holly."

"Well while we were up there, Mum asked me to sit down next to her and then pointed out a chest that was full of Dad's belongings."

"Well I did know about the chest," said Holly, "Mum mentioned the fact that it hasn't been opened for 14 years."

"Well, Mum tried opening it, she said there was something in the chest that she wanted me to have." Mum was struggling to open it as if it had been nailed down. She asked me to give her a hand because she was finding it difficult to get the lid open. Thinking it was going to be a demanding task to open, I placed my hand on the lid ready to force it open. To my amazement, the lid just released itself from its firm grip. Mum was just as surprised as me as to why the lid suddenly decided to open."

"This sounds really spooky Toby," said Holly with a scared look on her face. Mary was just keeping quiet for the time being, letting Toby tell his story.

"As the lid slowly opened, and I would say no more than an inch, I heard a whoosh-type noise and could feel a kind of coldness embracing me. Unfortunately, Mum was completely oblivious to it all when I asked her. She said she didn't feel anything and didn't hear anything."

"Mary, give me your hand," said Holly, "I will feel more comfortable if I can feel you next to me."

"Anyway, to continue," said Toby. "Mum and I were up in the attic for no more than about 30 minutes before we decided to come back down: football boots, photo of dad, wristwatch, all these wonderful things that belonged to our father were now in my room. Later on that night, I felt myself struggling to get some sleep; I was woken up by what seemed like a human voice in my room, it was over in seconds, and then I must have fallen back to sleep before I knew, it was morning and I could see the light of day was peering through my window."

"Were you not scared Toby?" asked Holly.

"Not really, however, it wasn't until the next night when the fun started, that's when I become really frightened." You could cut the air with a razor-sharp knife, even Mary was becoming frightened at the way Toby was telling his story. Toby continued once more. "That night, and completely unexpectedly, I was again woken by the same sound as the night before. First of all, the photo of our father fell on the fall causing me to sit bolt upright in bed. Shortly after that and still bolt upright in bed, I heard that familiar voice, except this time it was louder and clearer." Holly was now squeezing Toby's hand with a vice-like grip as well as Mary's; frightened to even breathe.

"I could see a Ghostly figure appearing in the dark near the foot of my bed, I knew it resembled a person, but whom, I had no idea. Seconds later, the spirit became vocal, he started calling out my name.

"Toby, Toby, it's your father, please don't be alarmed. Alarmed! He said; I was petrified. He continued by saying, when you opened the chest Toby, you let out my spirit, the spirit that has been locked away for 14 years. We chatted briefly, but for no more than a few minutes about this and that before I could see his spirit fading away back to the land of the living dead."

"Toby is this really true?" said Holly, "it sounds like a fantasy, something that you have made up. You are going to have to stay out of the school library and be careful what you read in the future. Why are you doing this to yourself?"

"It's got nothing to do with the school library Holly, nothing at all." Just then, Mary thought it would be better if she was to say something.

"Oh, it's true all right," said Mary giving her side of the story. "Just like tonight, Toby invited me to stay over, he needed to tell someone; he needed to get confirmation that it wasn't a fantasy or dream, just like you said, Holly."

"So that is why you stayed over then Mary?" said Holly, "it's all falling into place now." So what happened on the second night?"

"Well on the second night and with Mary present, our father showed himself once more," said Toby. "To be perfectly honest Holly, I wasn't sure if he would appear again, especially with Mary in my room."

"You can imagine how I was feeling," said Mary, "You are probably feeling the same way now, than the way I was feeling then Holly."

"Well Dad was now explaining more about how spirits operate," said Toby. He said that they can see us all the time, with discretion of course, and he will be there for us if we need his help. He also mentioned free will and the fact that he can't mess around with free will. However, what he can give us is advice and courage, but we are the ones that have to make our own decisions."

"Wow!" said Holly, "have you spoken to him again since?"

"Yes, quite a few times Holly. You know the football boots that were in the chest; well they have a magic power, why do you think I was playing so well, it's the boots Holly." It was difficult for Holly to take on board all the information that Toby was filling her head with, it would be better if she could talk to her father herself. "So do you think it would be possible for me to speak to my father tonight?"

"Well we will have to wait and see Holly, there are sometimes when he doesn't appear, even if I want him to; as he decided to point out to me one night, he still has a life to lead, or in his case, maybe not. He did mention that he did have a life, even in the land of the living dead."

"Why don't we just act as normal for a while," said Mary, "and that doesn't mean have a party, I just mean do the things we would normally do, try to forget about Ghosts and spirits for the time being."

"Normal, you want us to act as normal Mary? I don't think I will ever again be able to act normal after what you and Toby have just told me; "said Holly.

"I understand where you are coming from Holly, but to be perfectly honest, I think that's a great idea that Mary has suggested."

"So what do you suggest we do then?" said Holly."

"Why don't we have a game of something," said Toby.

"I spy with my little eye something beginning with G," said Holly. "Ghost, there you go, that's that game finished."

"Now you are just being stupid Holly, said Toby. "What about a game of Scrabble? That should take our mind off things."

"Fine by me, said Holly."

"You can count me in too," said Mary.

"Ok, then that's settled," said Toby. Toby got the Scrabble board out ready to start the game; sat on the floor, the game began with Mary having her go first. "FIST," said Mary feeling ecstatic with her four-letter word, 7 points."

"Well done Mary," said Toby, "let's see what I can do, 'FISH' for 9 points. Holly, you're up next."

"Ok,' GHOST' for 9 points," said Holly gleefully; "goes with the theme I thought."

"Very clever Holly," said Mary. "Ok then, I will go with 'SPIRIT' for 8 points."

"Ooh get you, Mary," said Toby looking surprised. The board was now looking very haunting as Toby also got in on the act with words like 'PRESENCE', 'SPOOKY', 'CHILLING' and 'CREEPY'. With the game now in full flow, everyone had forgotten about what the topic of conversation was about some two hours ago; but things were soon to change. Holly was just about to have her go when suddenly! She felt and saw one of the Scrabble tiles slowly moving without anybody touching it.

"Did you see that? Did you see the tile move?" yelled Holly with a wow factor look.

"Yes," said Mary and Toby, feeling spooked.

"There's another one moving," said Holly looking terrified. Holly Toby and Mary were now drawn toward the activity that was being displayed on the Scrabble board. Toby glanced over to his bedside table to see if there was any movement from his father's photo frame; not even a slight movement could be seen. As the tiles rearranged themselves the word was becoming a lot clearer now. 'TOM' was the word that was correctly spelt. "Tom!" said Holly, "Tom was the name of our father." More tiles were now moving around the board under their own steam. The letter's R.V.S.I A.T., were rearranging until the word Travis could be seen.

"I can't believe what I have just witnessed," said Holly in a state of bewilderment.

"Quiet for a second everybody," said Toby. "Dad, Dad, are you here with us, if you are please show yourself, Holly would love to talk to you." Holly was not expecting Toby to ask their father that question and was ill-prepared for what happened next.

"Are you there Holly?" said a voice from a distance.

Holly screamed at first causing Toby and Mary to jump on the bed and hide under the quilt, leaving Holly on her own. Within seconds Holly sprang onto the bed and under the quilt; a single bed had now turned into a King size bed for three people.

"Bloody hell Holly," said Toby, "you scared me to death. Just relax and answer him before he thinks we are kinky with alternative motives."

"I'm not complaining," said Mary smiling.

"Holly, get out of the bed now," said Toby putting his elbow into her rib cage.

"On yer bike Toby, you get out of bed?"

"I'm not sure if you have noticed Holly, but I'm the one in the middle, I can't move, Mary is practically in my trousers."

"Oh yes please Toby," said Mary.

"Mary will you behave yourself please," said Toby feeling disturbed by Mary's comments."Toby had just about had enough of the situation so decided to kick Holly out of bed. With Holly now sprawled out on the floor nursing a few bruises; it was now time for Toby to take control once more.

"Holly just speak to Dad will you, he won't bite your head off."

"Ok I will, but don't blame me; I just got spooked by it all. When you read about it in books you don't think for one minute that it can possibly happen to you."

"Well go on then Holly," said Toby. Holly took a deep breath and was now ready to talk to her dad.

"Yes, I am here, is that you Dad? Sorry, I got spooked, hope I didn't scare you."

"Yes Holly, it's your father, and no, you didn't scare me, well maybe be a little at first, but I can forgive you for that." Holly's emotions were now getting the better of her as tears could be seen running down the cheeks of her face. Suddenly, Holly's father appeared in the room. It was now time for Holly to ask the questions. "Can I touch your face Dad?" asked Holly tearfully.

"Unfortunately not, you can stretch your arm out towards me, but you won't be able to feel me. The only way you can get to feel me is if I transport my spirit into a human body. You will get the same feeling from me as if I was still alive."

"Can we do that Dad? Can we?"

"Well I think it is something you will need to discuss, it can be very emotional and startling at first Holly, maybe another night; feeling your arms around me again would be wonderful Holly."

"What about mum?" how do you think she would feel if I mentioned that I had spoken to you?"

"Let's give it a little longer too Holly, let's wait until we all feel that the time is right to tell her, I think she has enough going on in her life at the moment. I can see that she has taken a shine to another man."

"What! Another man, she has kept that quiet, and who might that be Dad?"

"Now that will be telling Holly, however, please don't discourage your mother if that's what she wants, she should be allowed to get on with her life; 14 years is a long time to wait Holly."

"Well after tonight, when can we talk again Dad?"

"Well I haven't got any plans to go on holiday soon," said Tom laughing. "Whenever you are available, whenever you need to talk to me; if I hear your cry for help, then I will do my utmost best to be there for you." Holly was full of all sorts of questions until she was feeling exhausted.

"Ok, I think it's time for me to go to bed now Dad, I'm getting so tired."

"Yes, that's a good idea, Holly, I could see you yawning, I think I will turn in myself, us spirits have to sleep sometimes as well you know. I will catch you all again, bye for now," said Tom.

"Bye Dad," said Holly and Toby,

"Bye Mr Travis," said Mary. Seconds later the room was feeling as empty as a flushed toilet.

"I cannot believe I have just been talking to my father," said Holly.

"Well mum's the word, well at least for now," said Toby in a kind of threatening way. "Not a word to anyone, we will know when it is the right time to tell Mum. I wonder who it is that Mum has got the hots for."

"Toby Travis," said Mary, "you can't use words like that, at your mum's age you don't say who as your mum got the hots for, that is something we would say at our age. You would say, and say it in a romantic kind of way; I wonder who my mum has taken a shine to."

"You obviously don't know my mum well enough yet Mary."

After a long night, it was time for bed, in Mary's case, time to go back home.

The next morning Holly decided to walk with Mary and Toby to the bus stop, giving them time to discuss what they intended to do about telling Rose.

"What about Saturday evening?" said Toby; "we could meet up at my house, let's say about 8-ish."

"I'm ok with that," said Holly, "what about you Mary, can you make it Saturday?"

"Don't see any problem there Holly; I washed my hair last month."

"Very funny Mary, I take that is a yes then."

"Yes, it is a yes, Holly."

"I would love to give my dad a cuddle, would you mind if dad's spirit goes into your body, Toby?"

"Well, that's a question if I ever heard one Holly. I'll be scared, I don't mind saying, but yes, ok Holly, if that's what you want."

"Yes, it is Toby."

"Wait a minute, do I get a say in the matter?" asked Mary feeling left out from the conversation.

"What's the problem Mary?" asked Toby.

"It's just that we really don't know what we are getting ourselves into Toby. Letting your mum know is one thing, but allowing a spirit to enter your body is something else. I'm not sure I feel comfortable with it."

"Well, I understand where Mary's coming from," said Holly, "the decision will have to be yours, Toby."

"I'm fine with it Holly, and as for you Mary, yes I want to do it, I trust my father, you'll have no reason to be scared."

Back at Lilly Pink School, it was now Holly that had to keep her mouth closed, even though she would have loved to have told her close friends. Meanwhile, back at Lakeside Secondary School, Toby was now more concerned about the game tomorrow. It would be Toby's first competitive game, one that he wanted to be on the winning side. As soon as Toby arrived home that evening, he made sure his boots along with his football shirt and shorts were neatly packed into his bag; losing them again wasn't an option. Friday morning arrived and Toby's mum was certainly not going to miss an opportunity to get a glimpse of Andrew again. "Will I be allowed to watch you play tonight Toby?"

"Well yes, I think so, I never really gave it any thought. If there are any issues that you can't watch, then I will phone you. Basically, if you don't hear from me, take it that it's ok to watch."

"Ok Toby, either way, I shall be there to pick you up at 5. 30."

"Ok, mum." Toby stepped outside his front door with his football bag slung over his shoulder waiting for Mary to arrive.

Just then, he was greeted by Bob and Brenda's collie dog Poppy. "Hello Poppy, hello girl," said Toby giving Poppy a cuddle. "How's it going, Poppy?" Poppy was all over Toby with excitement, in fact, she was that excited she was like a dog with two tails. Just then Mary could be seen exiting her house.

"Hi Toby," you are looking full of the joys of spring today."

"I'm just giving Poppy a super hug, such a gorgeous friendly dog."

"Well I hope you have saved a hug for me Toby, don't you go using them all up on Poppy."

"Of course, I won't come here Mary; I have saved the biggest one for you." With Toby's attention now fully on Mary, he forgot all about the excitable Poppy. As Toby unwrapped his arms from Mary he turned around and was shocked to see Poppy walking into the dangerous busy road without a care in the world. "Poppy No," could be heard as Toby ran towards Poppy with distress written all over his face. An approaching vehicle was now just seconds from a collision with Poppy. Toby tried in vain to protect Poppy from certain death as the screech from the tyres could be heard down the avenue. Mary was now hysterical as she stood there watching Toby being knocked over the bonnet of the car and into the road. Rose, Brenda, Bob, and Mary's mum were now all rushing to Toby's side with Mary now bearing down on Toby with tears in her eyes, all Toby was concerned about was whether or not Poppy had been injured. "Yes, yes, she is fine," said Mary reassuring Toby, "Poppy is fine thanks to you."

"Toby, are you ok?' said his mum shaking like jelly and in a state of shock.

"What's happened Mary?" said Brenda standing next to Bob.

"Toby has been knocked down by a speeding car. He tried to stop Poppy from getting run over and ended up getting run over himself." Bob and Brenda were inconsolable knowing that it was Poppy that had caused the accident.

"Don't put any blame on Poppy," said Toby groaning in pain. "Poppy was just doing what any dog would do; it was just an unavoidable accident." Toby's injuries were not looking life-threatening but Rose thought it would be better to phone for an Ambulance, just in case there were other injuries that were not visible. It took about 10 minutes for the Ambulance to arrive to the relief of everyone standing around. So what's your name then?" asked Dave the medic.

"Toby, Toby Travis," answered Toby.

"Wow! The same name as my colleague."

"Your colleague is called Toby Travis?"

"No," said Dave laughing, his name is Toby, not Toby Travis."

"Oh right, now I understand."

"Looking at your injuries I would say you have probably had harder knocks playing football Toby. However, your mum was correct in phoning for an Ambulance, you just never know. We will get you on a stretcher and then get you to the local Hospital. On arrival, you will be taken into the accident and emergency and a doctor will see you. You are more important than Royalty now Toby,"

Toby's spirits were lifted as he was driven away in the Ambulance. On arrival and after seeing the doctor, Toby's diagnostics were a bruised ankle and a few cuts and grazes, nothing a little tender loving care couldn't fix.

"There you go Toby," said the nurse. "Just keep the bandage on around your ankle and then it will need changing every morning; I will also give you some painkillers to be taken only if you feel you need to."

"Will I be able to play football tonight?"

"I'm afraid not Toby, if you are feeling better in a week's time then yes, but don't go at it at 100mph." Toby was now allowed to go home and get some well-deserved pampering from his friends and family.

"Toby, I will call the school to inform them that you won't be in for the next week and that you will have to miss the football match tonight.

"Ok Mum thanks, I'll tell you what though, Mr Symonds and Mr Mann won't be too pleased."

"Well tough, that is not going to happen; they will just have to find someone else to take your place. Where's my phone, have you seen it, Toby?"

"Your phone is staring at you, it's on the table."

"So it is, I'm not with it. I better put on my posh accent."

"Hello, Lakeside Secondary School for boys how can I help you?"

"It's Mrs Travis here, my son Toby Travis, unfortunately, won't be in school for the next week. He has been knocked down by a car, luckily, he has not suffered too many injuries; bruising on his ankle and a few cuts and scratches."

"I'm so sorry to hear that Mrs Travis, I shall inform his form teacher."

"Well thank you so much, could you also inform Mr Symonds and Mr Mann, Toby should be playing for the school football team tonight, and I'm afraid that's not going to be possible."

"I will do it right away Mrs Travis, thank you for calling." Back in the gym the phone rings, Mr Symonds is given the bad news.

"Andrew," shouts Nick.

"What's wrong?" said Andrew.

"Toby, Toby Travis, he won't be able to play tonight."

"You're joking Nick, tell me you're joking."

"Wish I was Andy, his first competitive game and what does he do; gets injured. We will just have to manage without him, hope he will be ok for the semi-final of the four counties cup."

"How did he get injured, Nick?"

"Well by the sounds of it, it seems like he had a lucky escape. He had an argument with a car, and Toby came off second-best. Apparently, he was trying to save the neighbour's dog from getting run over."

"Sounds like he had a lucky escape, did he manage to save the dog?"

"Yes, Toby and the dog are fine, it's just Toby's ankle that's bruised."

Back at home, Bob and Brenda popped around to offer them sympathy. "So sorry Toby, hope you get better soon. We have brought you a get-well card and some chocolates to take your mind off your injury."

"Aww, thank you Mr and Mrs Wilkinson, so kind of you, said Toby feeling a little sore." Bob and Brenda spent a good hour chatting to Toby; probably because they were still feeling a certain amount of guilt. In the evening Mary and Lucy were all over Toby like a persistent rash; Mary because she was in love with him, and Lucy because she had nothing better to do. "Would you like me to tuck you into bed later Toby?" asked Mary.

"No Mary, it's only a bruised ankle, I think I can manage that part of getting into bed on my own." Lucy just smiled at Mary with a kind of 'Bravo for you Mary', nice try. Mary and Lucy didn't stay too long, they were under strict instructions from Rose; she wanted her little boy to rest.

Saturday morning arrived with Toby getting breakfast in bed, "I'm off to the laundrette shortly," said Toby's mum, "only working till lunchtime, is there anything you would like me to get you?"

"Wouldn't mind a football magazine please mum?"

"I will call in at the corner shop and get you one on the way home. In the meantime Holly is at home if you need anything, failing that, give Mary a call."

"I'm sure I will be fine mum, now get off to work."

"Careful Toby, you're not too big to get your backside tanned."

"Holly, can I have a word please," said Toby from his bed.

"Be with you in a second Toby." Minutes later Holly was sitting on the edge of Toby's bed "What do you want to talk about Toby."

"Tonight, we were supposed to be telling Mum about Dad, even though Dad said to leave it a bit longer, at least until he feels Mum is ready to be told, and also, we were going to allow Dad's spirit to enter my body. Well, we can't do that now; I'm definitely not feeling up for it."

"You're right Toby, we will have to leave it until another day; maybe next Saturday would be better."

"I'm still not overly comfortable with telling Mum Holly; however, I know we have got to tell her at some point."

"Well that's settled then Toby, providing nothing of any importance comes up, then next Saturday it is."

"I will send Mary a text and explain to her, she will understand," said Toby.

"Ok, I'm going downstairs now Toby, if you need anything; give me a shout."

"Thanks, Holly, will do."

Meanwhile Rose was arriving at the laundrette to find it was really busy; being Saturday would have had something to do with it. It was quite a while before Rose Hilda and Marge could get a break. "Come on then Rose, get that kettle on, Marge get the mugs out, ordered Hilda."

"Yes sir," said Rose standing to attention."

"So how's Toby feeling today Rose?" asked Marge.

"I have left him resting in his bed, his ankle is sore but with a little bit of luck, he should be back on his feet by the end of next week. He was really lucky not to be killed. I'm going to take the week off next week Hilda; I think it would be better if I spent some time with Toby."

"Yes, that's a good idea Rose; we will manage," said Hilda sympathetically, "give him our love, and wish him a quick recovery."

"Will do," said Rose. He should have been playing football last night for the school team; the last game of the season. All I know is if they won last night, they would have had a chance of winning the league."

"So did they win?" asked Marge.

"I've no idea, not seen anyone from the school, probably will find out on Monday or sometime next week."

"Well let's hope they won; that will cheer Toby up." Just then a familiar face entered the laundrette, a face that Rose recognised. "What are you looking at Rose?" said Hilda.

"That man who just came in, I'm sure it's one of Toby's football coaches."

"What's his name then?"

"Andrew, Andrew Mann, I met him at a football training session last week. Do you remember when I collected Toby's boots from you last week Hilda?"

"Yes, how can I forget that Rose, the panic on your face will stay with me forever?"

"Well, I got chatting to him while I was waiting for the training session to finish."

"I'll tell you what Rose, he's a good-looking guy; I can see why you remembered him. if I was 20 years younger, I would give you a bloody good run for your money."

"Hilda! stop being so smutty It's nothing like that; stop making something out of nothing will you."

"So stand there and look me in the eyes and tell me honestly you don't find him attractive; you need your eyes testing Rose."

"I did not say that Hilda, and I certainly don't need my eyes tested thank you. Yes, I suppose he is good-looking if you put it like that. He's Toby's football coach for heaven's sake."

"So what's the problem with that?" said Marge, now getting in on the scene.

"Just listen to you pair; we are not having this conversation, now let's drop the subject." Rose just continued with her work until she heard a voice saying

"Rose, how you are?"

"Oh, hi Andrew," said Rose trying to sound surprised. "How are you?"

"I'm good thank you Rose; I didn't expect to see you here today, are you getting your laundry done?"

"No, I work here part-time, what about you?"

"I'm just bringing the football shirts from last night's game to be washed."

"Oh, we were just talking about that a few minutes ago, how did they get on last night?"

.Well, unfortunately, the lads lost 3-1, it means they finished second in the league."

"Oh dear, so sorry, Toby will be gutted when I tell him."

"Well if Toby had been playing, I'm pretty sure we would have won, we certainly missed his skill. How is he by the way, is he on the mend?"

"Very sore, should be back on his feet by the end of next week if it takes it easy."

"Well that's good news, tell him we have got the four counties semi-final in two weeks' time, and he will be playing. Unfortunately, the not-so-good news is, we have been drawn to play the same team that we lost to last night in the semi-final, and it's away at their school.

"What school is that then?" asked Rose.

"Darcy High School in Chester, they're a very good team, a bit dirty but they have plenty of skill."

"I will pass the message on Andrew as soon as I get home; that should cheer him up no end."

"Because we are playing away, we will be travelling by coach on Saturday morning, it's about an hour away. There will be room for supporters to go as well, not sure if you would like to attend Rose, we could do with as much support as we can."

"Er, I can't see why not, I'm pretty sure if I ask Mary and Holly they would love to come along too."

"Well I hope you don't mind me asking, but who are Mary and Holly?"

"Oh I'm sorry, no of course I don't mind you asking. Holly is Toby's older sister, and Mary is Toby's girlfriend and neighbour."

"Neighbour girlfriend, you will have to bring me up to speed on that one Rose."

"I'm sounding so vague, aren't I? I am so sorry. Toby has been going out with Mary now for about a month or maybe a little longer. However, Mary has been our next-door neighbour for about ten years." They are almost like brother and sister, that's why it seems a bit strange that they are going out with each other, that aside; Mary is a lovely girl and I would never stand in their way."

Rose had now opened up a little bit about her private life, but still knew absolutely nothing at all about Andrew; however, that was soon to change. Rose ran her eyes over Andrew's hands; "*not a ring to be seen on any of his fingers,*" she said to herself. Without trying to be too intrusive, Rose asked her first question of many to come. "We don't normally see too many men in the laundrette, it is mainly women. It's nice to see that some men take some responsibility for the running of their household, most men think that the house runs itself; well done for you."

"Well like I said, these are the football shirts from the game last night, so I am accountable for cleaning them and getting them back nice and clean." With Rose hoping for a little more information, like, "*I don't have a wife;*" she decided to be a little more direct with her next question. "So I suppose your wife will be glad to get you from underneath her feet for a few hours won't she?"

"Well, I guess I will never know Rose."

"Why's that then Andrew?"

"Well if I ever decide to get married, I will let you know."

"Oh so sorry, I didn't mean to pry," said Rose getting the answer she was fishing for. Andrew decided to open up to Rose to cut out all the unnecessary questioning. He could sense that Rose was feeling deeply uncomfortable with all her questions; it felt like an interrogation like he was on trial. "I actually live on my own, never really had any serious relationships; not met the right woman as yet. At my age of 38, you would be correct in thinking that I might be married. My career was too important to me, after leaving school I trained to be a sports teacher as well as playing football for my own town. At the age of 22, I managed to get a job at Sir James Talbot high school in Shropshire. I was there for 5 years. After that, I moved here to Cheshire to take up an equal role working alongside Nick Symonds, the other PT instructor. What about you Rose?"

"Well, how long have you got Andrew? Yes, I am single, 41 years old, my late husband Tom passed away at the young age of 30. He was diagnosed with a tumour on the brain; he died on the operating table. For the time being, I just tell the children it was natural causes. It happened just before Toby was born; some 14 years ago. Tom would have been 44 next month. We were only married for 7 years

"Wow! I'm sorry to hear your tale of woe Rose, and so sorry to hear about your late husband. I think now I'm the one that feels uncomfortable."

"Well don't be Andrew, it is sad I understand, but as I said, it was 14 years ago."

"Well maybe we could go out for dinner one evening or maybe you can come around to my place.... but obviously, only if you feel comfortable Rose. Then, then maybe we can find out more about each other, how would you feel about that?"

"Well, first of all, all this has come as a bit of a shock. I mean to say, less than an hour ago I was driving to the laundrette, and now, well I'm being asked out on a date.

"I am so sorry Rose, it was very wrong me, it wasn't meant to come across like I was asking you out on a date, please accept my apologies.

"Well, maybe I should be the one apologising to you Andrew. It sounds like I'm not being very diplomatic when it comes to trying to get my point across. So yes, it can't do any harm; it would be a nice change from my normal routine."

"Well that's wonderful Rose, I will look forward to it. What about next Saturday evening? Maybe a restaurant for our first date...listen to me, our first date...it sounds like something that we would have said 20 years ago."

"Yes, that would be nice, said Rose, "I will look forward to it." Andrew and Rose exchanged phone numbers so they could keep in touch with each other over the coming week. Rose managed to divert her attention away from Hilda and Marge for the rest of the morning, she just wasn't ready for a good old grilling; well at least until there was something more set in concrete to tell them.

CHAPTER 7

WILL ROSE FALL IN LOVE?

During the next week, it was much of the same with Toby now starting to put more pressure on his swollen ankle.

"How's your leg feeling Toby?" asked his mum.

"A lot better now mum, I think I will take a bike ride to the corner shop if you don't mind."

"Well just be careful not to put too much pressure on your ankle, you can pick up some milk while you're there."

"Will do mum." A nice sedate bike ride of about ten minutes saw Toby arrive at the shop.

"Hello Mrs Callaghan," said Toby.

"Toby, how nice to see you, how is your ankle?"

"A lot better now, thought the bike ride would do me good, need some exercise."

"When are you hoping to go back to school?"

"Well it's Wednesday today, so maybe I will have the next two days off and then go back on Monday. Is it ok if I start back with my paper round then as well?"

"Yes of course Toby. I was talking to Archie this morning and he said that he will still pay you for this week."

"How kind of him, please thank him from me."

"Of course I will Toby. How are things with you and Mary?"

"Really good, will it be all right for Mary to come round tonight, my mum will be fine with it, especially now that I am feeling better?"

"Yes, I will tell her when she gets home tonight, I'm sure she will look forward to seeing you. Did you come to buy anything or just for a chat?"

"Oh yes, nearly forgot, some milk please." Later that evening Mary made the long journey of 5 metres to Toby's' house, and then another ten metres to his bedroom, she must have been worn out by the time she entered his room.

"Hi Toby come here can give me a hug." The hugs were now turning into bed cuddles until they both rolled off onto the floor. Bang! The clatter was so loud that Toby's mum heard it in the living room.

"Is everything Ok up there Toby?

"Yes, sorry Mum; just tripped over my football boots."

"Well, just you be careful with that ankle of yours Toby." Mary and Toby were laughing quietly, trying not to give the game away. They were now like two love birds that were inseparable, with each day that passed their relationship was getting stronger and stronger.

"Do you fancy chatting to my dad tonight Mary?"

"Why don't we leave it tonight Toby, let's have some time to ourselves, maybe watch a movie on the TV."

"Yes, I'm fine with that, great idea Mary." Mary and Toby decided to watch a romcom movie from the comfort of the bed, how appropriate. Unfortunately for Mary, they both fell asleep; it was only when Toby heard someone going into the bathroom that he woke up.

"Mary, Mary. Wake up, it's 2 in the morning." Mary was still half asleep still not understanding where she was or what she was doing. It took a few moments for the penny to drop and realise she should be in her own bed at 2 in the morning.

"My mum must have gone to bed not realising that we were both asleep in my room. You are going to have to sneak out quietly Mary," said Toby whispering. Mary managed to creep out of Toby's house without making a sound; minutes later Mary sent Toby a text to confirm she had safely got back into her bed without her mum or dad knowing. The following day Toby decided it would be a good idea to get out of the house again. His mum was having the morning off from the laundrette, so it gave her an opportunity to do her food shopping and for Toby to come along.

"Toby, can you get me a trolley please?" asked his mum.

"Here you are mum, is this one ok?"

"Yes Toby, as long as it is empty and hasn't got someone else's shopping in it, then yes, it's fine." Rose put her handbag over the front of the trolley for safe keeping and allowed Toby to push it: Bread, milk, tins of Beans, cereal, butter and six bottles of wine because they were on sale.

"Why do we need the entire shop's stock of wine Mum?"

"Don't be so rude Toby; it's on sale, so may as well stock up while I can." Toby had never tasted alcohol in his entire life; however he was having wicked thoughts about what it would be like if he drank some; "*Mary and I, bedroom, a little tipsy, fun."* Just then, Toby's mum asked Toby to keep an eye on her mobile phone that was on top of her bag. It was Just in case someone tried to pilfer it. "Is my phone still there Toby?"

"Yes Mum, you don't need to worry, it's safe with me." Just then, Toby glanced down at his mums' phone to check it was still there. Toby noticed that a text had come through and couldn't resist seeing who it was from. First, he made sure that his mum was well engrossed in her selective shopping spree; pondering over which item to buy. Toby took the opportunity to see who the text was from. Toby was stunned and could hardly believe his eyes when he saw who the text was from. It was his PT teacher Andrew Mann. *Why would my PT teacher be texting my mum,* thought Toby. Toby was unsure of what to do; opening it was surely not an option, or was it? Toby could not resist the temptation, even though he knew his mum would know he's opened it. After checking his mum was not looking, Toby opened the text that read, *"Just checking we are still ok for Saturday Rose. I've booked us a table at the Holly Bush restaurant for 8 pm in Yelling. If you want, I can pick you up or I can meet you there, just let me know, Andrew."* There was no turning back now, Toby knew the contents of the text even though he wished he didn't; the only way he might get away with this is to delete the text before his mum finds out. Seconds later, and just before his mum turned around, he deleted the message.

"Ok there Toby?" asked his mum.

"Yes, of course, why shouldn't I be?"

"Just asking, you just seem a little edgy, in fact, you look like you've seen a ghost."

'I'm fine mum, just get off my case."

"Get off your case, what sort of language is that; that is no way to talk to your mother. I really don't know what they teach you at school these days Toby, they should have a lesson set aside to teach good manners.'

"We use it all the time at school, Mum."

"Yes, well maybe you do, but it is certainly not appropriate when you are talking to your mother. Imagine using it in front of Bob and Brenda, 'Get off my case,' Brenda," she would be mortified."

Toby found his mum's remark hilarious; "I wouldn't use it in front of Brenda, mum, that's a silly thing to say."

"Then you know how I feel now Toby; let's have no more talking like, I am not one of your school friends."

Toby and his mum finished their shopping and made their way home. Later on that day Toby again had some serious decisions to make; telling Mary, telling Holly and even telling his dad. Toby decided that he would go to his room and see if he could get hold of his dad; speaking to his dad first might be the answer to all the questions that were going on inside his head. Toby sat on the edge of his bed trying to get his dad's attention. Luckily for Toby, his dad was half expecting Toby to get in touch with him; after all, Toby's father sees what goes on all the time.

"What I can do for you Toby?" asked his dad.

"I would like some good advice Dad, some serious advice about a text I saw on Mum's phone today."

"Go on then Toby, I'm listening."

"Well, I'm not too sure if you will like what I'm about to tell you, Dad."

"I won't know until you tell me, so not to put too fine of a point on it, tell me your dilemma, Toby."

"Today I was shopping with Mum, she told me to keep an eye on her phone in case someone walked past and pinched it. I saw that she had a text so decided, and reluctantly I hasten to add, to check who it was from."

"Go on then Toby, tell me more, I'm all ears."

"It was from my PT teacher Mr Andrew Mann, I was shocked, I was thinking, why would my PT teacher be texting my mum."

"I hope you didn't open it Toby, that sort of information is not meant for you. It's your mum's private life."

"I'm so sorry Dad, yes I did; I just couldn't stop myself."

"First of all, I am not sure if I want to know what was in the text, it may have a bearing on the advice I might give you. Secondly, how do you think your mum will be feeling if she knew what you had done, she will never trust you again, would she? She will be absolutely beside herself with your behaviour. If you feel you need to tell me, Toby, then yes ok, I am all ears." Toby explained the text to his dad and the predicament he was in.

"Your mother is entitled to have a life Toby, and a private life at that. Again, as I said, free will is something I can do nothing about. If your mum wishes to have a boyfriend Toby then let her have her wish. How would you feel if she wouldn't let you see Mary?"

"I see what you mean dad, I would be devastated, but it's not just that, he is my PT teacher, my football coach."

"We can't help who we fall in love with Toby; Mary is your next-door neighbour and deep down, it could be making your mum feel uncomfortable. My advice is, wait and see what happens before you say something you might regret. Your main concern at this moment in time is keeping this news to yourself; telling even Mary or Holly could have severe consequences in the long term."

"Well I believe that is good advice Dad; that is what I will do."

"Oh and by the way Toby, please remember I am all for your mum seeing other men, as long as it isn't too many, only joking about the last remark. Is there anything more I can advise you on Toby?"

"No, that's been great thank you, Dad, will catch you again soon." It was now Friday and Andrew had still not received a reply from Rose so decided to phone. "Hello is that you Rose?" asked Andrew.

"Yes speaking, who's this please?"

"It's Andrew, Andrew Mann."

"Oh, how are you Andrew?" said Rose, "I should have checked the screen then I would have known it was you."

"Not a problem, and by the way, I am fine thank you. I'm just wondering whether you received the text I sent you yesterday."

"No, no I don't think so," said Rose feeling confused.

"Oh right I sent you a text yesterday at about 12.30, it said it had been sent 07828917357, that is your number isn't it."

"Yes it is; I would have been shopping at that time in the supermarket, with my Toby. I will ask him tonight if he heard my phone go off." Andrew explained the contents of the text and that he just needed confirmation that Rose was Ok with the arrangements. Rose said to Andrew that she would meet him there; with it being their first meeting, she did not want Holly and Toby to know, well at least for a short while.

Back home, Rose called Toby down from his bedroom; she had something she needed to ask him.

"On my way now mum," said Toby just dragging himself off his bed.

"Toby, I want you to be totally honest with me, did you delete a message off my phone when we were in the supermarket yesterday?"

"Come again, mum? Not sure what you mean," said Toby trying his best to look confused.

"Well, it's just that I had a phone call today, one of my friends was asking me why I didn't reply to their text yesterday.

"What! You think that I deleted your text, why would I do that?"

"Well I have no idea, Toby, you tell me."

"Who was it, mum?"

"Never you mind who it was, that is none of your business. "Anyway, you said you didn't delete any messages, so that is good enough for me. As far as I am concerned, that is the end of the matter." Toby felt quite relieved that the quizzing was over; although he still felt his mum knew he was telling a little white lie. Saturday arrived and Toby was taking an afternoon leisurely stroll through the park with Mary. They stopped at a park bench and decided to rest their legs for a while and to snuggle up to each other. Toby was being quite cryptic again with his questions to Mary.

"Do you think if your mum and dad were to split up, would they search for another partner?"

"My, my Toby, what sort of question is that to ask me?"

"Well, take my mum for instance; she has been single now for 14 years, I don't think she has even for one minute been interested in another man."

"Are you trying to tell me something, Toby?"

"No, I'm just wondering how you would feel if you were in the same situation as my mum."

"Well knowing my mum, I would say she would give it a couple of months, then more than likely; find herself a new boyfriend."

"So I wonder why my mum hasn't bothered getting a boyfriend then."

"I'm not sure about that Toby; only your mum can answer that question."

"I don't know how I would feel having a stepdad; he could never take the place of my father," said Toby

"No, he never could and never would Toby, I'm sure if your mum ever finds another man, he would understand that. I'm pretty sure your mum wouldn't get too serious with a man that doesn't respect her children. Are you sure there is nothing else you would like to talk to me about Toby; it was only when you were quizzing me about Ghosts a while ago that you eventually spilled the beans, you are very mysterious."

"No nothing else of any importance I can think of; oh by the way there is one thing. You know we are supposed to be telling Mum about us speaking to my dad tonight, well it will have to be put on hold again."

"Why's that Toby?"

"Oh, I'm just not feeling great; to be honest I'm really not in the mood tonight."

"Ok Toby; can't see that being a problem. Does Holly know?"

"Yes, I texted her earlier, she is fine with it. It will keep for another day, maybe next Saturday."

It was now early evening; Toby, Holly and their mum were sitting at the dining table eating tea. It wasn't long before the conversation turned to what everyone was planning on doing this fine Saturday evening. "What have you got planned tonight Toby?" asked Holly.

"I'm thinking of going around to see Mary for a couple of hours; shouldn't be late back though. What about you Holly, got any plans?"

"Yes, I'm off to see Amy, Amy Garvey; we are meeting up at the KFC in Yelling.

"What a great idea, would you mind if Mary and I joined you?"

"If you would like to Toby; then yes, can't see a problem with that, I'll be really nice to you and let you pay, can't say fairer than that, what do you say Toby?"

"On your bike Holly, actually, and just for your cheek, go on then, it will be my treat."

"Am I part of this conversation?" asked Rose feeling left out.

"Well you never go out on a Saturday evening Mum," said Holly, "the only time you go out on a Saturday evening; is when you go around to see Bob and Brenda."

"Well I'll have you know Holly; I am going into Yelling tonight; I'm meeting up with a friend.

"A friend mum, tell me more."

"Yes, a friend, we are going out for a meal, we are meeting up at the Holly Bush; nothing more, just a relaxing evening."

"Sounds very posh mum, you'll be telling me next your friend is a male."

"Well actually, it is a male Holly seeing as you're asking." Toby was looking rather sheepish, trying to stay out of the conversation. "Are you telling me you have a date, Mum?" Is that what you are telling me?"

"Don't sound too surprised Holly; there is still fire in my belly, it hasn't gone out yet."

"So who is he then? Do I know him? And not only that, where does he live?" Holly was so full of questions but the answers she was looking for were not forthcoming."

"You just enjoy your evening Holly; I will let you know more when the time is right." Within an hour the Travis family were hitting the town. Holly Toby Mary and Amy were tucking into their KFC, and Rose was getting to know more about Andrew over a glass of fine wine. "So tell me a little more about yourself then Andrew."

"I live about 3 miles away from the school in a little village called Ravensmore. I have lived there for roughly about the last 6 years and on my own before you ask."

"Never crossed my mind, said Rose chuckling."

"Anyway, in that time, I have been out with a couple of ladies, one of them was a school teacher but not from around here, and the other was a nurse at the hospital. None of them lasted more than a few months. My parents are still alive, living in a bungalow up north in the seaside town of Whitby. I have one sister and one brother, both older than me."

"And are you hoping to find the woman of your dreams and settle down?"

"I haven't given it a lot of thought Rose, if it happens it happens, if not, then maybe that's the way it is meant to be. What about you?"

"Well I won't say I am not interested in a relationship, but a little like you, I haven't really been looking for love since my husband passed away, although I must say, if the right man comes along then yes, I think I would consider a long-term relationship.'

"Does Toby know about our date tonight?"

"Well to be perfectly honest, I told Toby and Holly my daughter that I was off out tonight, but told them it was none of their business who it was; I am pretty sure though that Toby saw your text. I quizzed him about it only for him to strenuously deny that he had deleted it; I can always tell when he is lying."

"How does that work then Rose, I would like to know the secret."

"Oh, it's easy believe me, as soon as you see their lips move, they're lying." Andrew nearly choked on his food. "I must remember that one Rose. So are you going to tell Toby?"

"Yes, I think so, I have nothing to hide; I think the problem will be when Toby feels the need to tell his friends. For his own sake, he would be better off keeping it quiet.

"I have really enjoyed this evening Rose and would love to do it again sometime, what about you?"

"Well the minute I set eyes on you on the football pitch, I could just feel there was a connection there, you might call it women's intuition, I am not sure, I just felt there was something there, like the time I met Tom, my late husband. So on that note, yes, I would love to go out with you again, I have had a lovely time.

"Well, if it's not being too forward, what about coming to my house after the semi-final of the four counties cup next Saturday,

"That would be wonderful Andrew."

"I take it you are still coming to the match next week?"

"Yes, of course, wouldn't miss it for the world; where do we meet?"

"You will need to be at the school at 11 am. The game kicks off at 12.30; we should be back at the latest 4 o'clock. "

"Then that's settled," said Rose. A warm passionate kiss in the car park had Rose's head spinning before heading home. By the time Rose arrived back home, Toby and Holly were asleep in their bedrooms, so it would be Sunday morning before all the quizzing would start.

It was now close to nine in the morning. Toby and Holly were making their way down the stairs looking like they had been dragged through a bush backward. "Get yourselves sat down you pair of sleepy heads, breakfast is almost ready," said their mum. "How was your night Holly, did you have a good time?"

"Yes, just the normal stuff, nothing special."

"Never heard you come in mum; it must have been a late night."

"Oh about 11-ish I think, lost track of time as you do when you're enjoying yourself."

"So obviously you had a good night then mum."

"Yes I did thank you Holly; I had a lovely meal."

"So don't you think it's only fair that you tell Toby and me who you had a date with?"

"Ok Holly, you know what, I have just thought, it is going to be a lot easier for me to tell you who it is, rather than trying to keep it a secret. I just haven't got the time to be quizzed for the next half an hour." Holly and Toby waited with bated breath for their mum to tell them. "His name is Andrew Mann, Toby's football coach, it was only a casual date so don't try and spice it up and make more of it than it is."

"Wow!" said Toby as if to say he had no idea. Holly was even more shocked, but at the same time pleased for her mum.

"Well I thought it would be best for you both to know; keeping this information to yourselves might be the best way forward though. Imaging all of Toby's school friends knowing that Toby Travis's mum is going out with Mr Mann, it could be an uncomfortable situation to deal with, and possibly the same for you Holly."

"Yeah, I guess you're right Mum. Will you be seeing him again?" said Holly.

"Yes, on Saturday evening, he has invited me round to his house for dinner. By the way, I have said that we will all go and see Toby play next Saturday in the semi-final of the Four Counties cup. They have organised a coach for us all to travel in. I believe Mary is coming along as well. We should be back by 4 o'clock, that will give me ample of time to sort myself out."

"Yeah; well up for that mum," said Holly.

"Ok so let's hear no more about my private life."

"Ok," said Holly, "mum's the word."

"Ok by me too," said Toby. It was now Monday and Toby was returning to school after a week off, looking forward to seeing his friends. Could Toby keep his mum's relationship quiet? Well at least until after the semi-final. Would the school football team win through to the final? And is Mary asking too much of Toby? After all, he is only 14 with a lot to learn.

CHAPTER 8

TOBY'S PENALTY DILEMMA

"Hi there Toby," said Liam joyfully, "Long time no see, so nice to see you up and about again. How is your ankle now by the way?"

"Which ankle are we talking about Liam?"

"The one you injured Toby, you madman."

"Oh that one, well let us just say I can't wait to get back onto the football field again. It's feeling great thank you, Liam."

"Big game Saturday mate, semi-final, if we win that one, then we're in the final."

"Just hope I make the team; having a week off through injury can make it difficult to get back into the team."

"Now you are being stupid Toby. If we'd have had you playing the day you got injured, we would have won the league, even the football coaches were saying that."

"Anyway, changing the subject; how is your family?"

"They are all well thanks Liam; Holly has been looking after me like I was an invalid."

"And what about your mum, is she ok?"

"Yes, why do you ask about my mum?"

"No reason, just saying, how is your mum; nothing wrong in asking is there?

"No sorry, for sounding snappy Liam, I didn't mean to," said Toby finding it difficult to answer questions about his mum. Maybe Toby wasn't prepared for any questions about his mum; it would be something he would have to get used to. Back at Lilly Pink School, it was closing in on lunchtime. Mary needed to find Lucy, and quickly. She had a sensitive subject she needed to get off her chest, a subject she would feel uncomfortable talking to her mum about. After managing to find Lucy, they got themselves together in a quiet area away from the madding crowd. "So what is it that you want to chat about Mary?" said Lucy.

"Well, it's about Toby and me, we have been going out with each other for about 7 weeks now; I just get the feeling I want to take the next step but I'm not sure if Toby feels the same way."

"What, you don't mean sleeping with him do you Mary?"

"Yes, that's exactly what I mean. I will be 16 next birthday and then Toby will be 15, I just feel the time is right."

"Yes, I know what you mean, but at the moment you are still only 15 and Toby is 14. I'm not saying this sort of thing doesn't go on, and I'm sure you know what you are doing, but it's a massive step to take Mary."

"So are you saying you think I should forget about how I'm feeling, just forget about it ever happening, is that what you are saying?"

"Not exactly Mary, and just tone it down a bit, I am not your opponent in a boxing ring looking for a fight you know. I am just saying you would need to be careful that you don't push Toby away, you need to be careful about someone finding out; keeping it quiet from everyone else is also something you would need to take into account."

"Do you ever feel the urge to sleep with a boy at times Lucy?"

"Yes I do Mary, and maybe I am lucky in that sense that I don't have a boyfriend at this moment in time. What I mean by that is, I don't have to make that judgment call. If I was you, Mary, I would seriously think about what you are doing, maybe have a chat with your mum, maybe she is the one to give you advice."

"I would feel uncomfortable talking to her Lucy, I love her more than anyone would ever know, but talking to my mum about things of such a sensitive nature is not going to happen," said Mary feeling sad.

"Well if you still feel the same in let's say, a week's time, then the only thing you can do is discuss it with Toby, and then take it from there."

"Well, I was chatting to Toby this morning on the way to school, and he said his mum is going out on Saturday night and Holly will be staying over at one of her friends; someone called Amy I think, until Sunday.

"What! Toby's mum has finally got a date with someone Mary, tell me more?"

"No don't be daft; she is more than happy staying single. Anyway, as I was saying, I just think it's an opportunity for Toby and me to get more acquainted with each other."

"Well if you think Toby isn't interested in your advances, then don't push the issue any further; that would be my advice, Mary."

"Thanks for the chat Lucy; I feel better advised now, catch you later."

"Ok, see you later Mary."

At the laundrette, Hilda and Marge still wanted to know more about the mysterious man Rose was chatting to just over a week ago. With Rose taking a week off, Hilda and Marge were having withdrawal symptoms, they needed some gossip to brighten up their life.

"So who is this mysterious man then Rose? The one you were talking to a week ago," asked Hilda.

"Ok, to be honest, I was expecting this. I'll tell you anything to shut you up and put your mind at rest." Rose explained once more about her relationship with Andrew, about the date they had and about arranging to see Andrew again on Saturday.

"So where do you see the relationship going?" asked Marge.

"How do I know Marge, I have absolutely no idea where it's going, we will have to see. We have both agreed to take it slowly and see how it pans out."

"Well not before time Rose," said Hilda, we all need a man in our lives, well at least one that behaves himself; it sounds like you have got yourself a good 'un there Rose." With Marge and Hilda now knowing all about Rose's relationship with Andrew, it wouldn't be long before the whole of Yelling would be in the know.

It wasn't too long before school was out; Mary called at the corner shop to see her mum, just to see when she would be home. "Hi Mary," said Mary's mum, "you didn't tell me that Rose was seeing someone."

"I didn't know, Toby hasn't said anything to me."

"Oh, I didn't know that you didn't know Mary. Hilda from the laundrette popped in before and told me. Apparently, it's Toby's football coach Andrew Mann."

Mary was stunned into silence for once. "Mr Mann! Did you say Mr Mann, Mum?"

"Yes Mary, I did."

"I need to speak to Toby right away. In fact, I am not sure if Toby even knows. I will catch you later, Mum."

Back at home, Mary rushed around to Toby's house for confirmation of what her mum had told her. Mary didn't need to knock on the door anymore as she was practically part of the family. Mary ran straight up the stairs and into Toby's bedroom; this time and luckily for Mary, Toby was half decent as he lay on his bed reading. "Hello Mary, what a pleasant surprise; are you ok?"

"What are you reading?"

"It's a military book called Combats and Kisses. It's a true account of a young 16-year-old boy joining the Army and falling in love with a young Irish girl on the streets of Londonderry while he was serving his country; it's a brilliant read Mary."

"Maybe I will give it a go. Anyway, on to more concerning matters, is it true what I have heard Toby?"

"It depends on what you have heard, Mary. If you are asking if I have been cheating on you, then no, I haven't."

"No Toby, it's nothing like that, saying that, have you been cheating on me, Toby?"

"Of course I haven't, Mary, just joking with you."

"Well, what I have heard is that your mum is dating your football coach."

"I don't believe it," said Toby; "no one was supposed to know Mary. How the heck did you find out?"

"My mum was chatting to Hilda from the laundrette, she told my mum."

"Well, if Hilda knows, then the whole of the town knows. I was hoping to keep it quiet until the time was right to tell you, Mary."

"It's not your fault Toby; I just hope that it doesn't cause you any issues when the whole of school gets to hear about it."

"Same here Mary, that's why my mum and I wanted to keep it quiet, just to see how things developed."

"Well, I certainly won't be telling anybody, Toby. You can count on that."

"Don't worry yourself, Mary, the cat's already out of the bag; it won't make a big difference who you tell. Oh, by the way, we are just going to have to leave telling my mum about Dad once more. It just seems that every time we try to arrange it, something comes up. I'm sure when the time is right, we will tell her."

"Yeah, no problem Toby, I will catch you later."

It was Friday afternoon and the school football team was having a meeting at the school gym.

"Ok, listen in everyone," said Mr Symonds; "I have the team sheet here in my hand for the game tomorrow. I will be putting it up on the notice board for you all to read." Mr Symonds read out all the ones that were playing, including the substitutes. "Tomorrow is one of the most important days in the history of Lakeside Secondary School for Boys," said Mr Symonds. "Win tomorrow and we are in the final, a final that will be played at Nantwich Town's football stadium, a stadium that holds about 1500 people. I am sure you will all give it your best effort. As you well know, we will be playing Darcy High School in Chester, the team that beat us just over a week ago, 3-1. The coach will be leaving the school gates at 11.00 am tomorrow morning; I dare anyone to be late. All you will need to bring with you tomorrow are your football boots that you'll be playing in; shirts shorts and socks will be my responsibility. Mr Mann and I will be travelling in the coach along with any family members and friends who are coming along to support us. Have an early night lads, get yourselves plenty of sleep tonight; see you in the morning."

Toby decided not to meet up with Mary that evening; it would be the first time that they didn't see each other on a Friday evening. Toby was missing the chitchat that he was having from time to time with his dad, so thought he would call on his presence if his dad was willing. He didn't have to wait more than a few minutes before his dad was there in front of him. "Hi Toby, I thought you might be in need of a natter, especially with the game tomorrow."

"Yes, Dad; thanks for that. I not looking for any advice, I just fancy talking to someone, and with the fact I told Mary I would be better off not seeing her tonight."

"Well, how are things with you and Mary, then?"

"Fine Dad, it's just I have so much going on in my life at the moment, especially with my football. I feel that I am finding it difficult to sustain that spark that is required in a relationship like ours. I suppose what I am saying is, although I look forward to seeing Mary, I am not bothered either way."

"I suppose we could have a chat about the birds and the bees, then Toby."

"The birds and the bees, no I don't think so Dad, I know what I am doing, I just need to get that buzz factor back again; I'm pretty sure I will have it back soon. Once the football match is over, I will hopefully be in a better state of mind."

"Well, if you need a shoulder to cry on 'so to speak', then I don't think I am doing anything tomorrow night."

"Always the joker dad, however, I will hold you to that"

"I'm at your disposal, Toby."

"Well, actually, I have got something planned for tomorrow night. Mary is coming round in the evening with the fact that Holly is staying with her friends, and mum is also off out on a date."

"A date Toby? Tell me more."

"Oh sorry, I meant to tell you that Mum has finally met someone else. I have only just recently found out myself; my suspicions are now confirmed. It's Mr Mann, my PT teacher."

"Listen, Toby, I'm pleased for your mum. I have no issues with that. Give her my love when you see her."

"And how am I going to do that, Dad?"

"You mean you haven't spoken to your mum about me yet? I thought the cat was already out of the bag."

"No cat, no bag, no anything dad, you know I haven't told her yet. I have just not been able to find the right moment."

"Then maybe it's about time you find the right moment and tell her."

"I thought you didn't want me to tell her. I thought you wanted to keep it from her until the time is right."

"Well, it's been about 2 months, and now maybe I believe the time is right; I'm not saying she will believe you. When you feel the time is right, let me know, and we can work something out as to how we are going to do it."

"Sounds like a plan, Dad; that would be great." Toby was now feeling totally recovered from his depression after talking to his father; within minutes, and wrapped up in his duvet, Toby was away with the fairies.

It was now 10.30 on Saturday morning and everybody was starting to arrive in all sorts of modes of transport: Cars, Motorbikes, bicycles and even some on foot.

"Mary... would you mind if I sat with Liam on the coach?" asked Toby. "It's just that we can talk tactics, and not only that, Liam has got a way of making me feel less nervous than I know I will be."

"Oh right, I know when I'm not wanted. I'm sure there will be some other interesting boys on the coach. You sit with Liam if you like, see if I'm bothered.'

"Don't be like that Mary, I feel really bad now."

"Well, you started it, Toby, so I will finish it. Anyway, why should I mind you daft thing? Can you not see I'm pulling your leg? I will sit with your mum unless she wants to sit with someone else." Just then, Toby had a thought. *Sugar, I wonder if my mum is going to sit with Mr Mann.* "Why don't you sit with Holly?" I'm sure you have got things you can chat about; my mum can be quite tiresome to chat with at times.

"Toby....you can't say that about your mum," said Mary, laughing, "however I think you're right this time." Toby was now feeling relieved that his quick thinking had solved the situation. "Ok let's get you on the coach shouted Mr Symonds, I want all the team near the front so that I can keep an eye on you, and then everyone else can sit where you like." The team took to their seats as requested. Just as Toby was about to take his seat next to Liam, George Bulldog ventured into Toby's space.

"You," said George Bulldog, now inches away from Toby's face. "Ok Toby, this is a request for forgiveness. I feel like I have acted like a prat. You are actually a great guy... that said, it doesn't mean I want to share a shower with you. I was wrong about you; they say you should never judge a book by its cover; well that's exactly what I did." George gave Toby his hand to shake, and at the same time said, "You've got yourself a drop-dead gorgeous girlfriend; I wouldn't kick her out of bed." Toby didn't know how to reply to that remark; smirking at George was all he could think of to do. "Well, that was interesting," said Toby to Liam.

"Yes....He almost sounded human. He's not that bad, Toby; he didn't ask to be dropped on his head when he was born." Toby couldn't stop laughing at Liam's comment at the same time, trying to hide his laughter from George. Next to get on the bus were family and friends. Mary couldn't resist a quick rub of Toby's thigh as she manoeuvred her way past Toby. "Mary, stop it," said Toby, wondering what had got into her. Maybe Mary was thinking more about tonight's activities and couldn't control her emotions. Mr Mann had to sit at the front of the bus; what that meant was that he had to be extra careful not to draw any attention to the fact that he was dating Rose. The engine of the coach started up; minutes later they were leaving the town of Yelling for their journey to Chester. With the radio on, everybody seemed in a buoyant mood, like they were off to the coast at Blackpool; would their optimism last as the coach got closer and closer to Darcy High School?

"Over there Toby," said Liam, "there's the school."

"Seems like there are going to be a lot of people watching from the touchline," said Toby, with the butterflies kicking in.

"Ok, keep your noise down everyone," said Mr Symonds from the front of the coach. "We are almost here now. When we stop, I want you to stay on the coach until I have established exactly where we are going, and that means everyone, not just the football team." With the minutes counting down, the bus entered into the school car park through the main gates and parked up. You could see some of the Darcy football team lads; staring and pointing at the coach that was no more than a couple of metres away from them. "They seem very hostile," said Toby, feeling as if World War Three was about to start.

"They're just putting on a front, Toby, nothing to worry about. Anyway, if they want to play dirty on the field, I will set Bulldog on them; he'll chew them up and spit them out," said Liam.

"Come on then, you animals," shouted Bulldog, with his nose pressed up against the window of the coach.

"Bulldog," shouted Mr Mann, "get yourself away from that window, save all your anger for the field; and that goes for everyone else." Tension was now at an all-time high as Mr Symonds stepped back onto the coach. "Ok, listen in," said Mr Symonds sternly. "All the players, I want you to follow me when I say, and make your way into the gym with your kit. There is a dressing room that is completely separate from the home team's dressing team where you can get changed. We have a good half hour before the game kicks off, which will give us plenty of time to talk last-minute tactics and then get warmed up. Mr Mann and I will be in charge of your behaviour. Do not let us down. You will be representing Lakeside Secondary School, and not only that, you have an obligation to the good name of the town of Yelling. Win or lose, let's leave with our heads held high." The players all nodded their heads in agreement.

"All you lot that have come to see Lakeside Secondary School play, I would like to thank you for your support," Mr Symonds continued, "Cheer, shout, whistle, scream and thoroughly enjoy yourselves; get right behind the team, however, no swearing, no booing, no having a go at the referee." That sort of remark had everyone laughing. "The driver will be staying with the coach so you can have access to the coach whenever you want. The football pitch is just behind the gym. Just follow the path and it will get you there. Ok, lads; follow me in an orderly fashion." Within ten minutes, the team was ready in all respects for a final brief from Mr Symonds and Mr Mann.

"Ok lads, gather around," said Mr Symonds. "It's going to be a hard-fought contest; I know for a fact that Darcy will not be holding back any punches. I don't want you getting into a battle out there; that said, it doesn't mean I want you to shirk a tackle. If you need to get stuck in; then get stuck in. George Bulldog, you are naturally a tough cookie, don't change your style, that's why you were picked for the team; leave your mark George by all means, but don't get sent off. Liam, keep your men motivated. I want to hear you shouting your demands to all of your team. William McMullan, make sure you keep close to Liam, give Liam options to pass the ball, look for the space to run into and then call for the ball; clear loud calls William. Toby, I'm going to give you free rein. If you see there is a pass on... then pass it... if you feel you want to take on your man, then go for it, Toby. You read the game really well. So far be it from me to tell you what to do; remember though, it is a team game.... don't be afraid to bring other members of your team into the game. Defenders keep a tight line, and if you are in any doubt, just boot the ball upfield or out of touch. Andrew, would you like to say anything?"

"Well, I concur with everything you have said Nick, get out there, enjoy yourselves, and let's get to the final lads."

"Ok let's go, come on lads, plenty of noise, and let's show the Darcy lot that we are no pushovers." As they took to the field, Rose Holly and her friend Amy, Mary and one or two others were all there cheering on the lads, and soon to be accompanied by Nick and Andrew. I suppose the game was more important to Andrew than him standing next to Rose. He needed to stay as close to Nick as he could, ready to shout out their orders. With everybody now on edge with their eyes fixed on the field, the game began. Lakeside Secondary School started on the front foot. They were playing some really neat football and it wasn't long before their first attack. The ball was played efficiently from defence to the forwards, pass after pass, until William ran into some open space. "Pass it through Liam." Liam's sublime pass was perfect for William, however, just as William was about to shoot, 'BANG!!!' William was pole-axed to the ground, causing him to roll around in pain. Mr Symonds and Mr Mann were apoplectic with rage. "Referee, get him off, that's not football," said Andrew, "shouldn't be on the same field as my lads. Did you see that, Andrew? He kicked him right in the Niagara's."

"God, that must have hurt. I can almost feel the pain myself; I bet it made his eyes water." Andrew and Nick were doing their best not to swear. After all, they needed to practice what they preached. The Darcy defender got booked and a stern ticking off from the Referee. "Free kick," said the Referee.

The free kick was right on the edge of the 18-yard penalty area. "Get ten yards back," said the Referee pointing to the Darcy defence wall. William Toby and Liam were standing over the ball trying to hatch out a plan. Andrew, Nick, and all the Lakeside supporters were now standing in silence; a huge chance to go 1-0 up and a great start to the game beckoned. The Referee blew his whistle, Toby ran forward at pace as if he was about to strike the ball, instead, Toby ran over the ball only for William to tap it to Liam. Liam struck a curling shot over the wall that was heading for the top right-hand corner; with the goalkeeper well beaten, it looked odds on that it was going to be nestled in the back of the net. BANG!! The ball hit the post and then was cleared away by the Darcy defence. "Unbelievable," said Nick, "so close."

"Just typical of our luck," said Andrew. "Great effort Liam, so unlucky, chin up lads, you're playing really well." The game was now 35 minutes in and not a lot to choose between the two teams. Both teams were having chances, however; the best chances were definitely falling to Lakeside Secondary. On 41 minutes with Lakeside Secondary looking more like scoring, they were hit with a sucker punch. A shot from just inside the area fizzed past the Lakeside Secondary goalkeeper. The ball hit the inside of the post and then bobbled over the line. There was rapturous applause from the sidelines from all the Darcy followers. Andrew and Nick could hardly console themselves; shaking their heads in despair, they just took a deep breath and waited for the half-time whistle. The final few minutes saw Lakeside Secondary playing it safe. 1-0 is a score that they felt they could come back from; 2-0 and their heads would have dropped. Finally, the whistle blew for half-time. "Ok Lakeside Secondary, let's get you in the changing rooms," said Mr Symonds, wanting to deliver his half-time team talk.

"Listen in lads, you are playing really well. We shouldn't be losing but we are. I want you to keep playing the way you are; a little snappier and some crisp passing is all we were lacking. What do you think, Andrew?"

"Toby, I would like to see you making a few more direct runs at their defence," said Mr Mann. "I feel you have got the measure of their defenders, so let's see you get past them. As Mr Symonds said, much the same lads, it's yours to lose. Come on.... you can do this." It was now time to return to the field for the second half. Lakeside would have 45 minutes to turn things around. The sound of the whistle blew to start the second half of the match. It was Lakeside Secondary, once more starting on the front foot, attacking on all fronts like a well-drilled infantry unit. Toby could be seen skinning his defender and then with a perfectly measured pass, Liam was through on goal. Toby continued his run to the edge of the penalty area as the Lakeside team pressed forward onto the Darcy defence. Liam passed the ball to William, who in turn found Toby as he continued his run with a glorious cross; the post again came to Darcy's rescue, just like in the first half as Toby couldn't believe his luck.

Andrew and Nick could be seen shaking their heads from side to side once more. The longer the game stayed 1-0, the more rattled Lakeside Secondary was becoming. Gus Breeze and George Bulldog were now in the Referee's book. The game was reaching the 30-minute mark; only 15 minutes left for Lakeside Secondary to break down the Darcy defence. A free kick once more in the centre circle for Lakeside Secondary had the team still thinking we can still do this. Liam was becoming a lot more vocal now, shouting at Toby to get himself further forward. It worked a treat. The free kick was taken by George onto the head of Liam. Liam headed the ball into the path of Toby, who this time made no mistake with a thunderous fizzing volley into the roof of the net.

Andrew, Nick and all the followers were dancing on the touchline with delight." Could they now go on and win the game, or should they play it safe and go for extra time? There were now about ten minutes left, enough time for both teams to score a winner; playing cagey football is what both teams were doing now. One mistake though from either team could cost them the game. "Come on Lakeside Secondary," shouted Nick. "Push on, keep the ball, get back and defend as a team." There were so many conflicting instructions that it was causing confusion with his team; he just needed to let the lads play their own game. The 90 minutes were now up and Mr Symonds and Mr Mann were discussing how they were going to play out the 30 minutes of extra time, and at the same time, give their fingernails a good trimming. Suddenly, they heard a roar from his team. "What's going on Andy?" said Nick.

"Not sure," said Andy. "I think the Referee has awarded us a penalty."

"Are you sure?" asked Nick, looking towards his players, "William....William, is it a penalty?"

"Yes," said William clinching his fists. "Liam got fouled in the penalty box with a meaty challenge. I think he is injured, though."

"Liam normally takes the penalties," said Andrew, "I hope he can still take it. If not, I don't know who will be nominated to take it?"

"I've no idea," said Nick. Andrew and Nick were now feeling concerned. A few seconds ago, they were feeling animated and jubilant, and now, their joy had evaporated into thin air. Meanwhile, all the players gathered around Liam to see how bad his injury was. Liam tried to get to his feet, only to be seen hobbling around. Eventually, Liam was able to stand on his own but was in no position to take a penalty. "Toby, how do you feel about taking the penalty?"

"Are you sure Liam?" asked Toby, feeling humble that he had been chosen.

"Yes Toby, if I was relying on anybody to score from the penalty spot, then it would be you. "

"Well, Liam, because you have put your trust in me, then yes...I will take it." Meanwhile, on the touchline, Andrew and Nick could now see who had been given the responsibility. "Toby Travis, holy mackerel. Liam has nominated Toby to take the penalty," said Nick.

"Well, to be brutally honest Nick, I think that's the correct choice. It's hard to believe that about a month ago we were both saying that he had no chance of making the team and now... well he is about to take a penalty that would see Lakeside Secondary School get to the final of the four counties cup for the first time." Everyone was now out of the penalty area; it was Toby against the goalkeeper. Rose, Holly, Amy and Mary, along with Andrew and Nick, were now all huddled together on the touchline. The whistle was blown for the penalty to be taken. Toby was doing his best to concentrate and not to be put off by the goalkeeper waving his arms around like a windmill. Toby started his run of about ten metres; first of all slowly and then picking up speed as he got closer to the waiting ball. With a memorial thunderbolt of a shot, the ball hit the back of the net.

The force Toby hit the ball with was sheer power. Even if the goalkeeper had got his hands to the ball, it would have probably taken him into the net along with the ball. Seconds later, the final whistle was blown; Andrew and Nick were doing cartwheels along the touchlines. Their team had done it, they had reached the final. Liam was the first to congratulate Toby on his performance throughout the game. "Well done Toby, fantastic penalty. I never had any doubt."

"I just hit it as hard as I could, so glad it went in." It was difficult to get away from highlighting the wonderful collative unit assembled and coordinated by Mr Symonds and Mr Mann.

"Toby...Toby, over here," shouted Mary excitingly. Everybody on the team was a born hero; there wasn't one single member of the team that wasn't getting hugs and praises from their family and friends. A firm handshake from Mr Symonds and Mr Mann for each and every one of the team had them feeling swollen with pride. "Ok lads," said Mr Symonds, "get yourselves into the changing rooms: showers, kit packed away, splash on your smellies, then on to the coach; no smellies means you're walking back." All families and friends were now on the coach as the team made their way out of the gym; cheers aplenty from everyone as the team stepped onto the coach. Meanwhile, back at Lakeside Secondary School, one or two of the teachers, along with some family members, were waiting, hoping for some good news. "Here they are now," said one of the teachers. It was almost impossible to hide the excitement that was venting out of the coach. It was so obvious that it was the news everyone wanted to hear. "Well done Lakeside Secondary, so proud of you all," said the School Head Master Mr Bamford. Among all the excitement, Andrew managed to drag himself away from the crowd. "Rose, can I have a quick word?"

"Hi Andrew, yes, of course you can. Sorry, it's been difficult to chat with all that was going on."

"Just checking we are still ok for tonight."

"Naturally, so looking forward to it, 8 o'clock wasn't it?"

"Yes, that would be fine Rose, would you like me to pick you up? I have a top of the range two seated bicycle?"

"Me on a bicycle Andrew, yes, I bet you would love that. Actually, I was thinking of getting a taxi to be honest," said Rose, "four wheels and an engine; I thought we could both have a drink then. What do you think?"

"That is a great idea. Makes a lot more sense. Here's to a wonderful evening." Mr Symonds could be seen glancing over towards Andrew with a look of suspicion on his face. Maybe it would be something he would be asking Andrew on Monday morning back at school. It was now early evening at the Travis household. Holly was already on her way to Amy's and Toby's mum was getting changed for her night out with Andrew. Would Toby subside to Mary's advances? Could there be love in the air for Rose? And finally, what would be the chance of Holly dating Toby's best friend, Liam?

CHAPTER 9

A LOVE TRIANGLE

It was 7.30 and Rose was putting the finishing touches to her more than suitable dress. "You are looking very elegant mum; but do you not think that dress is a little short mum?" said Toby.

"Don't say that Toby, do you really think so?" asked Rose looking in the full-length mirror. "Mary was wearing a skirt that was no more than about 6 inches below her waistline the other night when she came round; so what's the difference?"

"25 years is the difference mum; anyway, that's the fashion these days for that age group."

"I feel really offended now Toby, you certainly know how to make me feel uncomfortable, you have really upset me."

"No Mum, I didn't mean to offend you, it came out all wrong. What I meant to say was, I have never really seen you in a dress that short before; your dress looks stunning."

"Well, I don't know how you have managed to dig yourself out of that one Toby; next time just put your brain into gear before you say anything."

"Put my brain into gear, that wasn't exactly very tactful Mum; now it's me that feels offended."

"No, you are correct Toby, it wasn't. Please accept my apologies."

"Apology accepted, and yes, Andrew will be knocked off his feet when he sees you tonight. He's a lucky man."

"Aww, thank you. I like it when someone sheds light on my youth, that is very grown up of you Toby; recognising that a woman always needs to look her best and.... that a woman likes nothing more than a compliment from a man. It's obviously a quality you inherited from your father."

"Like father like son, hey mum."

"Come here, Toby and give me a hug," said Rose with a huge smile on her face. "I shouldn't be too late back tonight; if you have any problems just phone me."

"Yes mum, you don't need to babysit me anymore, but thanks anyway. Mary is coming around soon. We are going to watch a film together, and maybe have some food."

"There's a pizza in the freezer if you want, just don't burn the house down." Just then there was the beep of a horn. "Oh, that will be my taxi. Give my love to Mary. See you later Toby."

"Bye mum, enjoy your evening." The sound of the horn also alerted the next-door neighbour, Mary; she was off her bed quicker than you could say Toby Travis, and then in a flash, Mary was peeping out of the window. Mary got a glimpse of Rose getting into the taxi before it drove away. "I'm off to see Toby now, mum," said Mary, heading towards the front door at speed.

"Ok, enjoy your evening. Don't be too late back. Have you got your key?"

"Yes mum, you don't need to wait up, Bye." Seconds later, Mary was knocking on Toby's front door. "Hi Mary, come on in."

"Well, I will only come in on my terms, and they are if you promise to give me a kiss first, Toby?"

"Yes, of course, Mary, come here." This was the first time Mary and Toby had spent time alone under the same roof, so she was naturally not holding back with her embrace. "Cheese and Rice Mary; thought you were trying to crush me; I could hardly breathe."

"I just feel so excited that we are finally on our own."

"Well, mum said there is a pizza in the freezer. Do you fancy pizza?"

"Oh yes please, I love pizza; that would be lovely. Do you want me to give you a hand cooking it?"

"Well, yes, If you like, I don't think it's rocket science, Mary. I will tell you what, you can turn the oven on and I will put it in. Then when it is cooked, you can take it out of the oven, and I will switch the oven off. That way we can both say that we cooked the pizza."

"Ok Toby, do I sense some sarcasm in what you said?"

"Me sarcastic; can't believe you even suggested such a thing."

"I think you know what I meant. I just wanted us to feel like we are a couple doing things together."

"I know Mary; I should take things more seriously at times instead of making a joke out of everything."

"Oh no Toby, don't change the way you are, your sense of humour is a rare quality to have." Within what seemed to be a few minutes, the pizza was ready. "Do you fancy taking it to my bedroom and eating it there?"

"Yes, I'm fine with that; we can eat it sat on your bed."

"Well, considering I haven't got any chairs in my bedroom, I would say yes. That's a bright idea."

"You don't need to mock me, Toby, I was only saying. Anyway, it sounds exhilarating. Can't think of anything better I would like to be doing on a Saturday night than eating pizza with my boyfriend sitting on his bed." If only Toby knew this was part of Mary's plan to bring a little seduction into the bedroom.

Meanwhile, Rose had arrived at Andrew's house. "Hi Rose," said Andrew giving her a kiss on the cheek, "let me take your coat." Andrew hung Rose's coat up on the hook in the hallway and at the same time, revealed Rose's beautiful blue sparkling just-above-the-knee dress. "You look amazing Rose, what a beautiful dress."

"Thank you, Andrew, you are looking very smart yourself. You shine up like a new penny."

"Well, thought I would make some sort of effort. Nice to get out of my tracksuit for a change."

"What would you like to drink?"

"Are we having wine with our dinner? If so, wine would be fine. Don't really like mixing my drinks. Doesn't agree with me."

"Yes, I understand, white or red?"

"White please Andrew; nice and chilled."

"Just take a seat in the living room. I will be with you in a second." Rose took a seat on the two-seater couch at the same time, scanning the room. She was trying to gather as much information as she could before Andrew returned. "Here you are," said Andrew, offering Rose her drink in a gentlemanly kind of way. "What are all the trophies for?"

"Oh, nothing special. Five of them are football trophies, those three over there are for rugby, and those over there are for judo."

"Judo," said Rose, looking surprised. Isn't that a dangerous sport? Don't you have to throw people and kick them?"

"Andrew almost choked on his wine at Rose's remark. Well, it's not quite like that. You can kick them if you like, but then you would be disqualified; kicking your opponent doesn't have any place in Judo. You are probably getting confused with the art of Kick Boxing, but yes, the idea is to throw your opponent onto the mat that you fight on."

"Without trying to sound rude, were you any good at Judo?"

"No, you're not being rude. But to answer your question, yes, I would like to say I was good at Judo. I was the North of England Champion once." Rose was impressed with Andrew's sporting adventures, not that Andrew was trying to electrify her; he was just answering her questions. "So where do you see yourself in five years, Andrew?"

"You mean, do I have a hidden agenda?"

"Well, I think we all need to map out our future Andrew, otherwise we become inactive, and we get up in the morning without anything to look forward to; that's surely not a healthy prospect."

"Too true Rose, I would like to think that in the next five years, I could be a top Judo coach, and on the home front, I must admit I haven't given that too much thought. Maybe I should think of settling down."

While all this was going on, Holly was having a lovely girly night with Amy. "Holly... isn't it about time you got yourself a boyfriend?" asked Amy.

"Try finding one that's worth having would be a good start, Amy."

"What about some of those lads that were running around on the football field today; don't tell me they didn't have you drooling Holly."

"Well, to be perfectly honest Amy, Liam Fenwick is a bit of a dish, he's got an arse like an onion."

"Arse like an onion, what do you mean by that?" asked Amy chuckling.

"It's an arse that makes you want to cry for." Amy almost fell over with laughter. "That is so funny Holly, I must remember that one."

"Anyway, I was chatting to him at Toby's birthday party, and yes, I was thinking about what girls like us to get up to when they get to our age."

"Really Holly, get you. Isn't he one of Toby's best friends?"

"Yes, imagine that Amy. Toby is going out with Mary our next-door neighbour, then there would be me going out with Toby's best friend Liam, and our mum is dating Toby's football coach; you couldn't script it Amy."

"Oh come on Holly, it would be amazing, you know it would. I'll tell you what Holly; let's get on to the social media site. If you are willing to message Liam, then I will also try find myself a boyfriend; you up for it?"

"Ok then, let's do it," said Holly. Holly and Amy were straight on to the social media site to see what they could find.

Back at Toby's house, Mary and Toby had managed to avoid burning the kitchen down and were now tucking in to their pizza in Toby's bedroom. "What film do you fancy watching Mary?"

"Something with a little romance and something with a good story would be nice. My friend at school said she saw one called 'Indecent Proposal', she said it was really gripping."

"Ok, give me a second Mary, I will check to see if I can find it. Here it is, got it."

"Shall we watch it lying under the quilt Toby?"

"You mean with our clothes on Mary."

"We don't have to keep our clothes on Toby, we can just keep our underwear on, why not?" we're on our own."

"Yes, but we should be behaving ourselves, what do you think your parents would say, Mary? I'm pretty sure they wouldn't approve?"

"But they're not here, we don't have to tell them, we are allowed some privacy you know. That's what falling in love is all about, sharing things together, our secrets."

"And don't forget about making pizza together."

"Oh yes, I had forgotten about the pizza." Mary had an answer for everything and managed to convince Toby to get undressed and lay with her under the quilt. "Can I have a cuddle, Toby, just before we start watching the film?

"Come on them Mary, anything to make you happy." They both turned inwards and wrapped their arms tightly around each other for a few seconds; at this point, the film was the last thing that was on Mary's mind until Toby said, "Come then, let's watch the film." Mary felt she was getting there slowly so agreed that watching the film was probably for the best.

Meanwhile, Rose and Andrew were now sitting down at each end of the dining table about to sample Andrews's cuisine. In a seductive kind of way, Rose smiled at Andrew over the rim of her wine glass; a gentle sip of her smooth silky cold white wine had Rose staring into Andrew's hypnotic blue eyes. Rose had certainly not lost her touch. Andrew was trying hard not to reciprocate the warmth he was feeling; taking it slowly and conversing between each bite was more pleasurable than rushing in at the deep end. "Did you enjoy yourself today Rose?"

"Yes, very much, Toby was incredible, so proud of him; I didn't think he had it in him."

"Well without trying to sound rude, he surprised me too. I wasn't sure of his ability to play for the school football team, but now, on a good day, he is by far our best player."

"You have a lovely house Andrew; you keep it really tidy and well organised; everything seems to be in its correct place. If you ever have children, you will know what I mean; trying to keep my house tidy is like asking KFC to look after your chickens." Andrew couldn't hold back his laughter, almost choking on his wine once more. "Yes I understand Rose, said Andrew still chuckling away. I hope one day to have a child; I am quite happy being on my own, I know exactly where everything is, maybe it's a kind of selfish attitude if everyone thought like me, we would become an endangered species." Again that remark had Rose laughing.

"Joking apart," said Rose, "does it get lonely at times Andrew?"

"Yes Rose, it certainly does, I suppose you can't have your cake and eat it. I would like to settle down with someone in the future Rose, like I have said before. Changing the subject, I will show you around the house after we have finished eating; I have made a Cheesecake for dessert if that is ok with you?"

"I worship Cheesecake Andrew; you can read my mind." If that were true, they wouldn't be sitting at the dining table right now. Back at Amy's house, Holly and Amy had managed to find Liam on Facebook. "Send him a friend request Holly on your phone, see whether he responds."

"Do you think I should?"

"Do I think you should? Of course, I do; send it now before I send it."

"Ok, there we go, it's sent."

"I wonder how long it will be before you get a reply, Holly."

"Maybe tomorrow, or even next week, we will just have to wait and see." Two minutes later Holly heard 'PING' on her phone. "Quick Holly; is it from Liam?" shouted Amy excitingly.

"Wow, I wasn't expecting that, yes it is, he has accepted my friend request."

"That's great, send him a message back."

"Ok, here goes," said Holly. *"Hi Liam, hope you are well, what are you up to?"*

"Not a lot, just resting my leg after the football today."

"I was watching the game, you played really well."

"Thank you, Holly, that means a lot. What are you up to?"

"I'm at my friend's house Amy, having a girlie night-in."

"I thought you would be out on the town on a Saturday night with your boyfriend."

"Nah... not got a boyfriend, what about you? I could say the same about you."

"No, I haven't got a boyfriend either Holly. As I said, I'm resting my leg."

"Ha Ha, very funny," said Holy, "You know what I meant."

"Oh do you mean do I have a girlfriend, then the answer is no, too busy with my football."

"Oh sorry, I didn't mean to pry ."

"You're not prying, anything that I am telling you, is because I want to tell you, otherwise I wouldn't say it. I tell *you what Holly, if you are free tomorrow, maybe we could meet up. When I saw you at Toby's birthday party, I enjoyed chatting with you, and if you don't mind me saying, I find you very attractive."*

"Wow, thank you for your kind comments, that would be lovely; where and what time shall we meet?"

"Well what about if I come around to your house about 2 in the afternoon, then we can go for a walk and get to know each other better."

"That would be wonderful Liam; I look forward to seeing you."

"Same here Holly."

"Wow! Can't believe it, Amy, I've got myself a date with Liam, we need to get you a boyfriend now."

Meanwhile, back at Toby's house things were hotting up. Mary was enjoying the film that had a sexual nature to it; the deeper Mary got into the film the more she was being moved by the sexual scenes. With Mary being much more mature than Toby, she decided to start playing footsie with Toby, to the point where her leg was now wrapped around Toby's leg. "What are you doing Mary?" said Toby being naive to Mary's advances."

"Just getting comfortable Toby, why, don't you like it?"

"Like what, you mean having your leg wrapped around mine, not really Mary." Mary was feeling annoyed with Toby's remark, her plan was not working like she had hoped. "Don't you have any feelings for me, Toby, why are you so cold?"

"Mary, I'm not cold, I am just not that sexually aroused like you."

"Well, maybe this will help." Mary started touching Toby on the inside of his upper thigh. "Mary; stop there right now." Toby jumped out of bed exclaiming, "Mary, that's enough I think we should get dressed now. Mary was very unhappy with the situation; this is the first time that Toby and Mary have had a major disagreement. "Thank you so much, Toby, you have made me feel so undesirable, I'm getting dressed then going home, don't inconvenience yourself trying to text me, my phone will be off."

"Fine Mary, I'm so sorry you feel that way, I think you are being very childish and unfair, we have plenty of time in our relationship for things to develop to a higher plane. Just give me a little more time, that's all I am asking." Mary had nothing more to say on the subject as she made her way home.

"You're home already Mary, I wasn't expecting you home until later," said her mum. "Is everything ok?"

"Yes fine mum," said Mary with seething anger written all over her face." I'm off to bed now, see you in the morning." Mary's parents just looked at each other shaking their heads as if to say. "*Just leave her alone until she is ready to talk.*"

As all this was going on, Andrew and Rose's short but sweet relationship was now blooming. "Lovely meal that Andrew," said Rose feeling fulfilled once more.

"Would you like some more wine?"

"Oh yes please, I think one more wouldn't go amiss; just getting a taste for it now." After recharging Rose's glass, it was now time for Andrew to take the next step. "Let me show you around the house."

"Oh that would be nice, thank you."

"Well you've seen the living room along with the kitchen and the dining room, so apart from the garden that is too dark to see, I will show you upstairs."

"After you Andrew," said Rose cheerfully.

"Well, this is the bathroom Rose, bath, shower toilet and sink. This is the spare bedroom that I use as a man cave; it's more of an office if I am being perfectly honest. And this is my bedroom, hope you like it. Rose couldn't believe how beautiful it was decked out: King-size bed, en-suite bathroom, walk-in wardrobe, it seemed like Rose's dream room. "Wow, it's so full of colour," said Rose, "I love the room."

"Have a look around if you want Rose, don't need to be shy."

"Me shy, I'm not shy, sometimes a little slow coming forward, but definitely not shy. It's just been so long since I was standing in a dark bedroom with a man."

"Well, how do you know if it was dark Rose?"

"Oh, you know what I mean Andrew; stop playing games with my mind."

"Let me turn the bedside light on, it might make you feel more comfortable. If you are not happy with the situation, then please, please don't go in."

"No Andrew, I have got to move on with my life, I can't hide behind the past forever. Just let me stand in the room for a few minutes; let me get used to the surroundings." Rose was now feeling more settled and walked closer to the bed. As she turned around Andrew was standing only inches away from Rose. She leant forward towards Andrew who in turn did the same. Rose's Heart missed a few beats as Andrew kissed her passionately.

"You don't have to go through with this Rose, I understand if you need more time."

"No Andrew, I want to." Rose and Andrew were really experts in lovemaking. They undressed each over with passion in their hearts, there was no rush. Within minutes of getting undressed, they slowly got into bed still holding each other. With the bedside light still on they made passionate love for the next hour. Rose was now on another planet, she didn't want the evening to end, but end it must. Rose decided to have a quick shower at Andrew's house before phoning for a taxi to take her home.

On arrival back home Rose knew nothing about Toby's and Mary's disagreement and the fact that Holly had a date with Liam. There would be lots to chat about on Sunday Morning.

Toby was first up followed closely by Holly and then within half an hour Rose emerged looking like she had been in a fight with a Rottweiler, and lost. "Morning my wonderful children," said Rose reaching into the fridge for some fresh orange juice. "How are we today?"

"By the looks of it, better than you mum," replied Holly.

"And what's that supposed to mean Holly?"

"Nothing mum, I take it you've not looked into the mirror this morning."

"No, I've just got out of bed; just need a couple of paracetamols."

"That won't alter the way you're looking mum, they're good for headaches, but as for the rest of your face, not a chance; remember the old saying mum, 'you are accountable for what you see in the mirror.'" Rose didn't even have the energy to make any kind of sarcastic reply as she made her way into the living room to say hello to the mirror. A loud scream could be heard bouncing off the walls from the direction of Rose. It was quite obvious now that she had understood what Holly was referring to.

"I take it you had a pleasant and enterprising evening Mum?"

"It was breathtaking Holly, could not have been better."

"Well, considering you are using words like breathtaking mum, I think I have finished with my questions."

"You are keeping quiet Toby," said Rose; "is everything ok with you?"

"Yes fine mum, to be truthfully honest, Mary and I had a little disagreement; our evening was over by nine."

"Aww, so sorry Toby, would you like to talk about it, talk to your little mumsy wumsy?"

"Well not just yet my beautiful Rosie Posie, maybe later. I'll see what happens today with Mary, I plan to pop around in the afternoon to sort things out."

"Ok, honey bun."

"Will you both cut out all this mumsy wumsy Rosie Posie and honey bun please," said Holly, "it's making me want to throw up."

"Don't be such a party-pooper, Holly, just having some harmless fun, isn't that right Toby?"

"Yes, mumsy wumsy."

"That's enough mum, no more please."

"Anyway, getting back to what you were saying, Toby. The number of arguments I had with your father when he was alive, I lost count, the fun part though is making up Toby; it's only then that you realise how much you are in love."

"Well, I'll let you know Mum." Just when Toby was getting his thoughts together, and everything was looking clearer after chatting to his mum, he was hit with a comment from Holly.

"I've got a date this afternoon Mum."

"Really Holly," replied her mum in a shocked type of voice. When was all this arranged?"

"Only last night, Amy and I were surfing the net and thought it was about time we had a boyfriend."

"Oh so it's that easy is it Holly, you fancy a boyfriend so you just go on to the net a get one?"

"Well when you put it like that, then yes, it can be that easy."

"It sounds like online shopping to me Holly, it has taken me 14 years to find a boyfriend, you found one in 14 minutes."

"Well, actually 5 minutes mum."

"So who is he? Does he have a name? Or is that something you don't need to know when you do this skiing thing or whatever it is called."

"Surfing mum, and yes of course I need to know his name; you just don't jump into bed without knowing his name mum, well at least his first name anyway."

"Holly, that's enough of that thank you."

"Sorry Mum, it's just that you ask some crazy questions. Anyway, just for the record, his name is Liam, and I fancy him."

"Oh so he does have a name then, Liam, yes I like that name. In fact, there is a Liam on the school football team, is that correct Toby?"

"Yes, he is the captain; he was at my birthday party if you remember Mum."

"Come to think about it, yes I do remember Toby, a good-looking lad if I remember correctly; what's his surname, Toby?"

"Fenwick, Liam Fenwick." Answered Toby

"Sorry Holly I got sidetracked, did you manage to get the surname of your date, or does that come later?"

"No, it doesn't come later mum; and for your information, his surname is Fenwick, Liam Fenwick."

"Wow, the same name as Toby's friend, how ironic is that?"

"Very Ironic mum, it's the same person, I thought you would have worked that one out already. It's Liam Fenwick, Toby's best friend."

"You have got to be having a laugh, Holly," said Toby choking on his breakfast.

"No, it's true, he's coming around at two this afternoon and then we might go for a walk." Toby was stunned by the news report. His mum is dating his football coach, his sister is dating his best friend and his relationship with Mary is on the rocks.

"Maybe we can turn 45 Primrose Avenue into a dating agency mum, maybe we can turn it into a thriving business. I can get some business cards made up; I can pass them around to some of the more discerning lads at school on Monday morning. Would you like some Holly? Maybe some of your more discerning friends would like a business card too."

"I shall have to ask them Toby, great idea of yours," said Mary sarcastically.

"No, it's not a great idea Holly, that's my point, now stop winding me up. You know I wasn't serious."

"Well that's my point, Toby, you joke around so much that even I don't know when you are being serious."

Toby had definitely lost the plot. That afternoon Rose had now sobered up and Liam was at the front door.

"Hi Liam," said Holly with a huge smile. Liam was actually 16 years old, six months older than Holly, and two years older than Toby. With that in mind, Liam greeted Holly with a quick but meaningful kiss on her lips. "Come in Liam," said Holly, "What do you fancy doing?"

"Well, as we talked about last night, I think it would be nice if we went for a walk. We could take a walk to the park; maybe get some takeaway food, something like that."

"Yes, I would like that Liam; that would be really nice." While Holly and Liam were getting to know each other, Toby was hoping he would have heard from Mary by now. Unfortunately, Mary was making Toby suffer in silence; there was no way that Mary was going to be begging Toby for forgiveness. In her mind, she felt it was Toby that was to blame, and that she was only doing what in most relationships would be classed as normal. Toby was only 14 years old and not ready for a more sexual connection, but Mary couldn't understand the age thing was a major concern for Toby. Would Mary and Toby ever get back together again is the question that needed to be answered. With the four counties football final coming up in the next two weeks, Mary wass the last thing on Toby's mind.

CHAPTER 10

TIME TO TELL MUM ABOUT DAD

It was Monday morning. Toby and Holly were getting ready for school when Toby just happened to see Mary getting into her mums' car.

"Are you walking with Mary this fine sunny morning Toby?" asked Rose.

"Well, by the looks of it, I would say no."

"What do you mean by that Toby?"

"I've just seen the back end of Mary getting into her mums' car, it's a bit of a giveaway isn't really Mum."

"Oh dear, just give her some time; I'm sure things will work themselves out."

"Well to be perfectly honest Mum, as much as I love Mary, I think I have enough going on in my life right now, more than you will ever know."

"Oh, you mean with your football?"

"Well that and the fact that Holly is seeing Liam, you are seeing Mr Mann my football coach, and also, oh it doesn't matter."

"And also what Toby, how can I help you if you don't come to me with your problems?"

"Have you got anything planned for Wednesday evening mum?" asked Toby.

"Not to my knowledge Toby, and if I have, I can easily cancel it."

"Well no matter what, even if something comes up Mum, can you make sure you keep it free? It's very important that we have a chat. Remember when it was my birthday and you had something you wanted to show me the evening before, well, now I have got something I would like you to see."

"Now you have got me feeling concerned Toby. I do like surprises but I'm not sure whether or not I am going to like this one.

"Well, now you know how I felt then don't you mum?"

"Fair point well made Toby; I will look forward to it. Now get yourself off to school before you are late."

Rose arrived at the Laundrette to be welcomed by Hilda and Marge waiting eagerly to find out how Rose's evening went with Andrew.

"Sit down Rose your brew is waiting," said Hilda. "so how did your evening go then.?" asked Marge.

"Well, it started with Andrew taking my coat off just like a gentleman would, and hanging it up in the hall. He offered me a glass of white wine and at the same time, asked me if I would like to take a seat on his two-seated couch.

"And then what happened?"

"Well he joined me on the couch if that's what you mean, and then we just talked for a while, getting to know more about each other and that sort of thing."

"Yes, it's that sort of thing we are talking about Rose."

"Behave yourself; we just chatted away as I told you."

"So what was dinner like? I bet he's a good cook, none of this ready meal stuff."

"Well after a few more glasses of wine, we went into his dining room. "We had a lovely roast meal that he cooked from fresh; it was followed by my favourite pudding, Cheesecake."

"So did you get romantic Rose? That is what I really want to know," said Marge.

"To be perfectly honest, yes we did. After the meal he showed me around his beautiful home; initially, he showed me downstairs, and then we went upstairs."

"Wow! This is getting juicy," said Hilda. "Did he show you his bedroom?"

"Of course, he did, along with the bathroom and his man cave."

"Oh, they call it a man cave these days do they, in my day they called it a tadger."

"What on earth are you on about Hilda? A man cave is a room where a man has all his toys, or whatever he wants to put into his room. It has nothing to do with what you are referring to."

"Oh I see, so it's not his, well you know what I mean?

"Yes, I do know what you mean, and no, it isn't Hilda, it has nothing to do with the male anatomy. Why don't you just come out with it Hilda, and ask me if I slept with him, that is what you are getting at isn't it?"

"I wouldn't dream have asking personal questions like that. Ok then Rose, did you sleep with him?"

"Yes, I did, and don't you dare tell anyone Hilda, or you Marge. I've got nothing to hide, but I just don't want my children to find out. I'll tell them in my own time, do you understand?" said Rose very forcefully.

"Yes of course Rose."

"Yeah, well make sure you do, just don't let it slip out anywhere."

"We are under oath not to say a single word, Rose, you can certainly count on that," said Hilda.

Back at school, Toby's first port of call was to find Liam. Toby was at a point now where he needed to clear the air with all that was going around him. Toby sent a text to Liam saying that he wanted to meet up with him at lunch break. As soon as Liam received the text, he knew right away what Toby wanted to chat about. Lunchtime couldn't come quickly enough for Toby. Liam and Toby found a nice secluded place on the grass bank by the school playground, somewhere where they wouldn't be disturbed.

Sat down and absorbing the ultraviolet sun rays, Liam and Toby were ready for war.

"Ok then Toby, I know what this is all about, so let's get started."

"Well yes, you going out with Holly would definitely be a good starting point, Liam." Toby was sounding very masterful as if something had finally dropped while he was asleep last night.

"Well let me explain Toby, before you jump off the handle. None of this was planned, and I know how uncomfortable you must be feeling, I would more than likely be feeling the same if you were going out with my sister."

"Oh you mean the sister you haven't got Liam."

"Yeah, ok Toby, you don't have to remind me, so let's say if I had a sister."

"Anyway, carry on with what you were saying."

"Holly sent me a text on Saturday evening, you know, just a sort of innocent text." We chatted for a few minutes and before I knew it, we had arranged to meet up. I have actually been contemplating for a while about asking her out on a date, and every time I thought about asking her, my thoughts were on how you would feel; the exact reason why I have been holding back. Last night she probably caught me off guard and before I knew it... well let us just say; the rest is history."

"What am I going to do Liam? Do you know my mum is dating Mr Mann the football coach?"

"Really? I had absolutely no idea Toby, when did all this happen."

"About two weeks ago, I've been trying to keep it quiet but it seems that the cat is out of the bag. Do you remember the training session we had on that Wednesday, well that's when they first met. My mum brought my football boots that apparently, I left at home; they got talking on the sideline and again, the rest is history."

"I'm so sorry Toby, how do you feel about it?"

"Not Happy, but again, it's something I'm going to have to get used to, aren't I?"

"Well they say everything comes in three's Toby, you're just another fine example of that saying, things can't get any worse."

"Really, you really think so Liam? Well, let me tell you something else that you might find interesting. Mary and I broke off our relationship last night. So just when you think things can't get any worse, I'm hit with the bombshell that you are dating my sister.

"I don't know what to say. I'll tell you what Toby, I'll tell Holly that I made a mistake; I will tell her that I need some time to think. I will say that until the four counties final is over, I will need to concentrate on that first."

"Liam, you will do no such thing. It is not your fault, you didn't know about my mum, you didn't know my mum was going out with the football coach and you certainly didn't know Mary and I had split up."

"So what are you trying to tell me, Toby?"

"I want you to carry on seeing Holly, you certainly don't need my permission, in fact, it also means I will get to see you a lot more as well.

"Well that's a big weight lifted off my shoulders Toby, thank you for being so understanding."

"Well I've got a lot of things to sort out Liam; this is the first of many, to be totally honest; I feel so much better now."

Meanwhile at the Lily Pink School for girls, Mary was chatting to Lucy. "Ok there Mary," said Lucy, "I tried phoning you yesterday but it just went to voicemail."

"That's because I turned my phone off, didn't want to be disturbed."

"Oh, well that explains it then. Any reason at all why you turned it off, or would you like me to start guessing?"

"Start guessing," said Mary, I will give you one guess that should be enough."

"Could it be Toby by any chance?"

"Correct; got it in one. Well, I might as well tell you before someone else does Lucy. I had a bit of a set too with Toby on Saturday.

"And may I ask about what about Mary?"

"What do you think Lucy? Remember what we were talking about last week, you know about taking our relationship to another level, well maybe, and regrettably I should have listened to you; disappointingly I think I've scared him off."

"Oh Mary, I'm so sorry, do you want to talk about it?"

"Not really, I just think that I have blown any chance of continuing my relationship with Toby. I just was not expecting him to react the way he did.

"What did you actually do Mary?"

"Well we were lying under the quilt in our underwear which he agreed with, but then I started playing footsie with him. He was sort of ok with that but not that comfortable. He asked me what I was doing and then when I explained, he then quite forcefully asked me to stop."

"And did you stop?" said Lucy feeling a little shocked.

"Yes of course, but then after a few seconds had gone by, I started to rub the inside of his thigh, I couldn't stop myself, Lucy, I was getting aroused by what was happening in the film we were watching. It was a wonderful feeling, Lucy. Unfortunately, Toby shot out of bed like he had been spooked by a spider. I was so angry; I just couldn't hold back and told him how immature he was."

"Immature, that's harsh Mary; you must remember he's only 14."

"I know you're right, that's exactly what Toby said. Anyway, it doesn't matter now; I quickly got dressed and went home, without even saying goodbye."

"So I take it you haven't spoken to Toby since your altercation."

"No, to be perfectly honest I'm not sure if he still wants to see me again, and also I'm not sure if our relationship is still worth pursuing. It was just like you predicted Lucy."

"Well I suppose I did warn you, Mary, it was a bit clumsy of you even though you mean well. It wasn't rocket science; even a blind Squirrel could find a nut. Maybe give it a couple of days, when you have both had time to think about it you might both see things in a different light." The school was now finished for the day and Toby was thinking of calling at the corner shop for some confectionery. Toby knew Mrs Callaghan would be there so felt very uneasy about trying to explain to Mary's mum about him and Mary. Toby made his way into the shop in a sheepish kind of way but ready for action. "Hi there Mrs Callaghan," said Toby jovially.

"Hi Toby, what can I do for you today?"

"I think a big bar of chocolate today, more of a treat to myself."

"What are you so buoyant about Toby; you sound like you are floating on air." Toby was actually trying to mask his depressing mood, Toby finally realised that it is far more rewarding feeling cheerful than feeling unhappy; Toby had definitely turned a corner. "Mary said you have had a bit of an altercation on Saturday, she was in a right mood when she came home."

"She'll get over it," said Toby smiling like a Cheshire cat.

"Oh, Ok Toby, you don't sound too bothered, I thought you would have been feeling down in the dumps."

"So did I Mrs Callaghan, but you know what, there are worse things going on in the world today than to worry about our little disagreement?"

"You are so right Toby, well said, you make a very good point." Toby took his chocolate and made his way home. Mrs Callaghan was left pondering with what Toby had said, she just stared out of the shop window until Toby was no more to be seen. Toby was feeling ready to take on the world now with his cavalier attitude. Back at home, Toby went searching for Holly.

"Holly, are you in your room?" shouted Toby from the foot of the stairs.

"Yes, come up, I'm just putting some clothes away." Toby made his way up the flight of stairs and into Holly's room. "You had a good day ?" asked Holly.

"Yeah, fine Holly thank you?"

"Did you see Liam today; you know just wondering?

"Yes, of course, I see him every day unless he's not at school. Are you asking me if I got talking to him, and what did he have to say?"

"Well yes, did he have anything to say?"

"Well, to cut to the chase, I actually text him and said I think we need to talk. We sat on the grass bank and chatted for about half an hour, about football."

"Football, oh right.... Nothing else then," said Holly.

"Oh, you mean did we talk about you and him?"

"Well I did wonder, so you never mentioned me then?" said Holly.

"I didn't say that exactly. Of course, we talked about you and him, that's what I wanted to talk to him about, we never even mentioned football."

"You arse Tony, stop winding me up. What did you talk about?"

"To be perfectly honest Holly, what you and Liam get up in your spare time is your business and none of mind. I must admit it though, when I first heard about it, it came as a bit of a shock. I think I can live with it Holly, in other words, I wish you more luck than I had with Mary."

"Thanks for that Toby, it means a lot, it just makes things more comfortable for me. Are you sure your relationship with Mary is over?

"Well, I would say definitely for now. I will probably wait until after the four counties' final and see what happens. Anyway, that isn't what I wanted to talk about. I was talking to Dad two days ago and we have decided to tell Mum." I have arranged it for Wednesday night, how are you fixed, Holly?"

"Well I had arranged to meet Liam; I will text him and say I can't make it as something has cropped up."

"Invite him round tonight instead, would be nice to see him," said Toby

"Yes ok, that's a good idea, I'll phone him shortly, and see what he says. "Oh by the way, what time tomorrow are we meeting up Toby?"

"Well, I was thinking after tea. We can meet up in my bedroom again; Mum is bound to feel uneasy, so we need to reassure her whenever possible," said Toby.

"Ok, suits me fine," said Holly "Can't wait to see mum's face, hope she doesn't become too scared and freak out."

"I'm sure she will be fine; anyway if the worse comes to worst, we can blame Mum, it was Mum that was wrestling around with the idea to open the chest. I will catch you later at tea Holly." Toby went back to his room to have a lie-down and at the same time checked his phone to see if he had any messages from Mary, just on the chance Mary wanted a chat. Although Mary was out of sight, she was without a doubt still not out of mind; it was going to take a while before Toby was to get rid of all thoughts of Mary. Within minutes Toby was snoring for Britain; it was only when he heard his mum shouting from the foot of the stairs that he came out of his coma. "Toby tea's ready, I'm serving it up now."

"Give it to the dog Mum."

"We haven't got a dog, Toby."

"Oh, in that case, I'm on my way mum; I just need to freshen up." Downstairs Toby was taken by surprise to see Liam sitting at the table next to Holly. "Oh hi Liam, I didn't hear you arrive."

"It was probably because the dog was barking.

"We haven't got a dog, Liam."

"Gotcha, I can't believe that you told your mum to give your food to the dog. Anyway, you were well out of it Toby, I could hear you snoring from Holly's bedroom."

"Sorry about that, I was so tired. Have you heard when the final will be taking place, Liam?"

"Should find out towards the end of the week, I was talking to Mr Mann today, and he thinks it will be on Saturday 4th May but yet to be confirmed."

"Who will it be against?"

"Not sure about that either, I think it will be against Helsby High or Great Sutton Secondary. It felt so strange having Liam around for tea but at the same time Toby was enjoying his company; something he would need to get used to.

Wednesday arrived and Toby had still not heard from Mary, in fact, he had seen nothing at all of her. He never saw her going to school, he never saw her arriving home from school, and the curtains from her bedroom window were giving Toby the impression that she was becoming a recluse, in the respect that they always seemed to be closed. It was now 8 pm. Toby and Holly were sitting on the edge of the bed in Toby's bedroom waiting for their mum to arrive. "Is it ok for me to come in now?" asked Rose from the foot of the stairs.

"Yes of course Mum, come up whenever you are ready." Rose made her way up the stairs and into Toby's room. "Sorry, there is nowhere to sit Mum."

"No problem, I'll just sit on the floor, Toby."

"Just wait there a minute mum," said Holly "I'll get you the chair from my dressing table, we can't have you sitting on the floor mum."

"Very thoughtful of you Holly, that would be nice."

"So what is all this about then? I'm very intrigued."

"Do you want to start Holly or do you want me to explain?"

"You can Toby; I will just fill in the blanks."

"Ok mum, here we go. Holly and I have been talking to Dad over the last couple of months without saying anything. The day you and I opened the chest that night in the attic was the day when we let Dad's spirit out, can you remember that noise I said I heard, and that kind of chill that ran through my body, well that was his spirit."

"Don't be silly Toby, that sort of thing only happens in fairy tales."

"The whole thing sounds like a fairy tale Mum believe me, but I am telling you now, it happened. If you remember Mum, I asked you a few weeks back if you believe in spirits and your answer was yes."

"Yes I know Toby, in some way I do, but I would never expect to see one, how can you sit there and say you've spoken to your father."

"It's true mum; tell him, Holly?"

"It is true Mum, for once Toby is not messing around. I didn't believe it when Toby told me, there was no way he was ever going to convince me. I felt the same feeling that you are feeling right now. I was absolutely bricking it when our father finally appeared in this room."

"Ok, even though I still feel it's as far-fetched as Leeds winning the FA Cup, I'm all ears. So what can I expect to happen now?"

"Well if you are sure you are ready to talk to our father, then I will turn the light down and call him." Said Holly

"So let me get this right Holly. What you are telling me is that you can get yourself a boyfriend in five minutes on your laptop, and now you are also telling me that within a few minutes, you can talk to ghosts. Is it really that easy Toby, you just turn the lights off and he appears?"

"Well yes, I suppose it is Mum; however our father is a bit of a joker, he likes nothing better than to wind me up. It wouldn't surprise me if he isn't hiding underneath the bed at this moment in time."

"How did you guess Toby," came a ghostly voice from underneath Toby's bed."

"Hocus Pocus," said Rose, squirming in her chair, it even startled Toby and Holly; no one was expecting this. Toby and Holly comforted their mum before she had a chance to escape from the bedroom. Tom now made himself visible to the room. "Rose you are looking so stunning," said her late husband in a romantic kind of way. "It is so wonderful to see you again, please don't be alarmed, Rose. I have never and never will stop loving you, you know that don't you?"

"Yes Tom and I have never ever given up hope of ever seeing you again, but I thought it would be when it is my turn to pass over to the other side, not like this. Can I touch you, Tom?"

"I'm afraid that the only way of doing that is if I allow my spirit to enter a living body. For now, I think we can do that at a later date; maybe when we are all more comfortable with carrying out this inner body experience. I see you have a boyfriend now Rose, good for you; carrying on with your life is so important. You don't need to be concerned about me knowing about what you get up to, as I explained to Toby and Holly; I have my own life to get on with in the land of the living dead."

"It feels so wrong now Tom, you know, seeing another man."

"Well what do you think I have been doing for the last 14 years Rose, I have had a few girlfriends, but none of them 'lived' up to your standards Rose; the relationship was pretty much 'dead' in the water before it even started."

"Always the joker Dad," said Toby, "I told you he was a joker mum, he never takes anything seriously. I love you so much dad, you always find a way of cheering me up."

"Oh, don't get me sniffling Toby, my spirit can't distinguish whether I am crying or peeing, the number of times I have pee'd myself when I thought I was crying; not a pretty sight."

"I love and miss you so much too Tom," said Rose.

"I love and miss you too Rose," Toby and Holly realised that their presence would be better off somewhere else. "Come on Toby," said Holly, "I think we should leave Mum and Dad to have some time together, they are becoming very emotional."

"I think you are right Holly."

Toby and Holly made their way into the kitchen and had a cup of tea while they waited for their mum to have a catch-up with their father. It must have been a good hour before Rose said goodbye to Tom and acquainted herself with the living again; that would be Holly and Toby.

"Are you ok mum, "asked Holly.

"Oh yes, thank you so much for bringing your father back into my life, in fact into our lives'. It feels so much like a family again."

"So glad we have made you happy Mum," said Toby, "to be honest, you handled it a lot better than Holly and I, we were so scared."

"Will you be speaking to Dad some more over the coming days mum?"

"Yes, he actually said he will talk to me in my own bedroom Toby."

"Well that's great mum, I'm pretty sure he will talk to you in your bedroom too Holly." Over the next few days, it was now becoming common knowledge to everyone that Toby and Mary had split up, Liam was dating Holly and Rose was seeing Mr Mann.

CHAPTER 11

FUN AND GAMES

Back at Lakeside Secondary School, the date for the four counties' final had now been confirmed. Saturday as 4th May, only nine days away, they would be playing Helsby High who won the trophy last year. The school football team was summoned for extra football training over the next few days. One of the sessions would be this Saturday in two days' time. The lads were told that it would be a 10 pm morning session at the school football field. Anyone not turning up or even turning up late would be in hot water; scrubbing their chances of playing in next Saturday's final. Saturday morning arrived, and after checking his phone, Toby noticed a text from Mary. She wanted to meet up with him to try and clear the air of what was obviously a misunderstanding. Toby sent a text back to Mary and agreed to meet up mid-afternoon; all seemed well until Mary spotted Toby outside his house about to go to football training. "Hi Toby, said Mary awkwardly.

"Oh, hello, so nice to see you again; how have you been keeping Mary?"

"Well to be perfectly honest Toby, I have been missing you; in fact, I've been missing you a lot. Have you got time for a quick chat?"

"I've only got a few minutes Mary, that's why I said this afternoon would be better for me."

"Ok, well maybe just a quick 5-minute walk around the block, if that's ok, please, pretty please, pretty pretty please?"

"Ok Mary, you have won me over again, you have my whole undivided attention."

"First of all I would like to apologise for the other night, it was very wrong of me to expect you to succumb to my advances. I have had time to think about my behaviour and realised that if the shoe was on the other foot, I would have hated it."

"Exactly Mary, I would have probably been nicknamed the Yelling Pervo, that's him, there he goes .... Pervert, should be ashamed of yourself, should be locked up and have the key thrown away." As much as Mary wanted to be serious, after all, her relationship with Toby was in the balance, she absolutely burst out laughing at Toby's well-over-the-top remark. "The Yelling Pervo Toby, the Yelling Pervo. Come here and give me a cuddle you mad man. I've missed all of your funny comments Toby; it feels like I have had a sense of humour failure over these last few days. You know what though Toby, you are totally correct. In these days of equality, we should be all treated with the same balance of fairness. Maybe women do get away with more meaningful crimes. What I am trying to say is, can a woman physically be charged with sexual harassment?"

"I've got absolutely no idea Mary; it is not the sort of thing we talk about at the dining table; I'll ask my mum tonight when we are eating tea."

"Don't you dare Toby, chuckled Mary; "you'll get me into trouble."

Anyway, that aside; thank you for being so understanding Mary, it means a lot to me. It has been difficult for me as well over these last few days; however, I suppose I have had a lot more on my mind with everything that is going on in my household. My house felt more like a dating agency, you know with Liam dating Mary, my mum dating Mr Mann, and also with the four counties football final next Saturday."

"Well Toby Travis, can I be part of this dating agency again, can I have a small share in the business once more?"

"Well that's certainly a strange way of asking me back into your life, I think I might have to consult with the other two shareholders first, see if they are willing to sell you some shares so we all have an equal share in the business. I think five pounds should do it."

"Well it feels like the flowers are blooming again Toby," said Mary feeling on top of the world. "I'll tell you what, why don't we meet up tonight, and I will bring you the five pounds for my share in the company. You and I, and Holly and Liam; we could go out for a Pizza. It would be a nice way of getting our relationship back on the road. And only if you promise not to seduce me, Toby, I've heard of people like you, in fact, there's a rumour flying around that there is a Yelling Pervo on the loose."

"Very good Mary, I wonder where you get your sense of humour from; I will do my utmost best to keep my hands firmly on my pizza."

"I've never heard it called that before Toby, that's a new one on me." Toby just shook his head from side to side. It was nice to see the banter returning between them.

"My God Mary, look at the time, you said 5 minutes, according to my watch I've literally got five minutes to get to school." Toby was now panicking and, in a race to get to school on time; being late could have severe consequences. As Toby arrived at the school gates, he could already see that in the distance the football training was in full flow. "Where the hell have you been Travis? Did you not hear what I said the other day?" said Mr Symonds.

"Yes sir, every word you said."

"So I may as well have been talking to a brick wall then, is that what you are saying?

"No Sir, I can explain, I left my house in plenty of time but my neighbour Mary saw me and needed to get something off her chest."

"I imagine it was probably her chest that had something to do with why you are late, am I correct Travis?

"Well, I suppose indirectly you could be right Sir. Mary and I had split up and she wanted to talk about getting back together again."

"I don't need to know any more Travis, get yourself changed and on to the football field, pathetic excuse. I will talk to you later." After a good two-hour session practicing all sorts of different tactics, Mr Symonds called time to the relief of the team.

"Liam, can I have a quiet word," said Toby. "Do you and Holly fancy meeting up tonight at my place and then eating out at Pizza Hut? Mary and I had a heart-to-heart this morning, that's why I was late. We have decided that maybe we both overreacted the other night so we kissed and made up, so to speak."

"That's brilliant Toby, so pleased for you both. I will call Holly now." Just then Mr Symonds could be heard close by.

"Travis, get over here now, I need a word."

"Best of luck with this one Toby, catch you later." Toby made his way over to where Mr Symonds and Mr Mann were standing. It would be very difficult for Mr Mann to show his true feelings on Toby's behaviour with the fact that he is dating Rose, Toby's mum. "Ok Toby, taking into account that you are amongst the best players we have, if not the best, we wouldn't want to lose you from the team; I'm sure the rest of the team would concur with that. You will make Mr Mann and I look stupid if we don't show any authority or discipline towards you. We have decided to put you on a warning, in other words, one more slip up Toby and you will not be travelling with the team next week, even though it will weaken the team. Would you like to say anything Andrew," said Mr Symonds.

"I would just like to say that I probably understand the reasons behind your late arrival today. We have all been there Toby. The fact that I am dating your mother unfortunately may seem to some of the other lads that the reason behind our decision, is for that reason; believe me, it isn't. Anyway, make sure when you talk to the rest of the team and you tell them you have had a lucky escape."

"Thank you, Sir," said Toby," thank you for being understanding."

"On your way now Toby," said Mr Mann. Toby trundled off with his head bowed to get changed and tell Liam what the outcome was. "He's a good lad is that Toby Travis," said Andrew to Nick.

"Yeah I know, let's hope he heeds our advice, I'm sure he will; we wouldn't want to travel to Nantwich next week without him on the coach. Anyway, it's Saturday, fancy meeting up in town later for a drink or two?"

"I'm actually seeing Rose tonight Nick; Saturday is really the only time we can meet up and have a drink or two."

"Well why don't you bring her along and I will bring my wife Linda."

"Sounds like a really good plan Nick, just give me a second and I will call Rose." Within a minute or two Andrew had his answer. "All settled Nick, I'll meet you at the Feathers at about 8, is that ok?"

"Look forward to it Andrew, I'll catch you later."

It was now 7 pm and Liam was just arriving at Holly's house. "Hi Liam," said Rose getting ready for her night out.

"Hi Mrs Travis, how are you this fine evening?"

"Never felt better Liam, thank you for asking. Holly will be down in a second; I saw you coming down the drive so I gave her a shout. Where do you and Holly plan on going tonight?"

"We are going to Yelling with Toby and Mary; we will more than likely end up in Pizza Hut."

"I didn't know they were back together again; when did all this happen?"

"Just this morning, Toby told me they had sorted out their differences."

"He could have told his mother first, tells me nothing that one. Anyway, so glad they are back together again."

"Are you out tonight Mrs Travis if you don't mind me asking?"

"No, I don't mind you asking at all Liam. Actually Yes, I'm getting a taxi to Andrew's house, sorry I meant Mr Mann, and then we are meeting up with Mr Symonds and his wife Linda, I believe his name is Nick."

"Well, I hope you have a lovely time Mrs Travis."

Thank you, Liam, I'm sure we will." Just then Mary arrived; making the living room look more like Piccadilly Circus.

"He is in his bedroom Mary, I'm pretty sure you know where it is," said Rose sarcastically. That sort of remark had Mary thinking if Toby told Rose about why they split up.

"Hi Toby," said Mary as she entered his room. "Did you say anything to your mum about the reason why we split up for a few days?"

"No, of course not Mary, I wouldn't feel comfortable discussing those sorts of issues with my mum, what do you take me for."

"I didn't think you would and I don't mean to pry, it's just when your mum made a comment about me knowing where your bedroom was, and the look she gave me, had me thinking that you had said something."

"Well now you know I didn't, come here and let's make passionate love on my bed."

"Toby, don't let's start all that again, stop teasing me, and stop winding me up. You know how the saying goes. If you are born with a silver spoon up your backside you are classed as a snob, you should have been born with a silver key up your backside Toby; you are always winding people up. I am more than happy to take things more slowly, particularly now we are back together again Toby."

"Yes I know, just a little bit insensitive from me, I was just trying to have a laugh."

"I appreciate it, Toby, here's to a wonderful evening."

Later on that evening at the pizza hut, the foursome were now having a great time telling stories and joking between each bite of their pizza and their soft drinks.

"Toby." said Holly, "should we tell Liam about our secret, I mean to say, even Mary knows, it doesn't seem right not to share the secret with Liam; after all, he's practically family now."

"I guess I'm ok with that," said Toby, with Mary also giving her approval.

"Toby Mary and Holly all leant forward into Liam's space making Liam feel like he was important. "Ok, what's all this about?" asked Liam. The storyteller began telling the story in a ghostly tone.

"Not last night but the night before.... three big Tom cats came knocking at the door, one with Whiskey one with Rum and one with a poker stuck up its bum." Mary and Holly were in fits of laughter at Toby's story; they were both expecting Toby to tell Liam about their father. Liam knew he was the subject of one of Toby's jokes but also found it hilarious.

"Toby Travis," said Mary, "I thought you were going to tell him about our other little secret."

"I was, but I just thought I would catch you all out with a joke."

"Well Toby, I think that we should tell Liam about the real reason we have a secret," said Holly.

"Yes, that's a great idea Holly," said Liam chuckling out loud. "Anyway, I don't know if I can take any more of Toby's inappropriate and disgusting jokes in front of two glamorous ladies." Eventually, Toby and Holly began to tell Liam about the fact that they are able to see and talk to their deceased father. It was very difficult for them to convince Liam, especially with the mocking type of mood they were all in; with that in mind, it would be up to Liam to believe whatever he wanted to believe. It was now time to head back home; what would be the chances of the foursome bumping into another terrible foursome making it an eight-some?

"Is that our mum over there?" asked Holly staring.

"Good God, yes it is," said Toby. "She is the only woman I know that staggers after a couple of Lemonades."

"Toby, you can't say that about your mum, wait till I tell her."

"Hi Mrs Travis," shouted Mary across the other side of the road.

"Mary, what are you doing, don't you dare tell her what I said."

"Then give me a kiss and I won't."

"You're impossible sometimes Mary, it's a good job I love you." Just then they saw their mum almost falling into the gutter. "Toby, Holly, how are you both, having a good night I hope?

"Fine mum," they both said.

"Looks like you have had a good evening mum," said Toby, "saw you almost fall off the kerb."

"Clearly not," said Rose slurring her words.

"I bet she tries to blame it on the shoes Holly."

"It's these bloody shoes, I won't be wearing them again in a hurry," said Rose slurring her words once more. It was a slightly more uncomfortable situation for Nick and Andrew, not knowing whether to joke or to be a little more serious; luckily for them, Toby Holly Mary and Liam were mindful of what they said. All in all, it sounded like everyone had a cheerful evening.

It was now Monday morning and after a hectic weekend, things were getting back to normal. Toby and Mary could be seen walking to the bus stop on their way to school like two love birds once more, and Rose was making her way to the laundrette to her part-time job. The only slight difference now was Holly would also be meeting up with Liam on the way.

All the talk was about the ever closer four counties final on Saturday; the love life of the Travis family was in some respect going to be put on the back burner. Mr Symonds and Mr Mann got all the football team together in the afternoon. They were all told to meet up in the gym and that all lessons for any member of the football team were cancelled for the rest of the day.

At the gym, the football team were waiting with bated breath and wondering why this mandatory meeting had been called. Mr Symonds and Mr Mann arrived in a more casual kind of way that had the team feeling that it wasn't going to be a rollicking they got.

"Ok gather round, and listen in to what I am about to say," said Mr Symonds. "I have spoken to the headmaster and he has given me a free rein to spend more time with the team all of this week. Every afternoon this week, you will be at my disposal along with Mr Mann. All other lessons that are on your weekly planner will be null and void." A loud controlled cheer went up from the team along with beaming smiles.

"As well as football practice and tactics, Mr Mann and I have been wondering if some of your parents could provide us with some help. "Whose parents have got a sewing machine and can also sew?" There were a few hands that went up but as for the rest, I don't think they had even heard of a sewing machine. "Ok, well the next question is; who is going to be brave enough to volunteer their parents into making some scarves and banners. We are looking for about 50 scarves and quite a few banners.

The scarves will need to be green and white stripes; some of them can be knitted and made out of wool or maybe some silk ones. We just want to create an intimidating atmosphere on Saturday; gain an advantage wherever possible. Toby and William, I noticed you had your hands up, come and see me after the football session. The rest of you can ask your parents to make cakes sandwiches sausage rolls, et cetera; we want it to be an unforgettable day." After the football session, Toby and William reported to Mr Symonds as asked to. "Ok Toby and William, I need to know where you live so that Mr Mann can drop off the material to your house early evening, and also just to double check that your parents are ok with the sewing." Even though Mr Mann was dating Rose, he still hadn't been to her house yet, something I'm sure he would be looking forward to. Later on that evening at Toby's house, typical Toby had forgotten to inform his mum that Mr Mann would be popping around, what a shock she got when she saw his car pull up outside her house.

"Toby," shouted Rose from the foot of the stairs. "Are you expecting Mr Mann, he has just pulled up outside in his car."

"Oh damn, yes mum I forgot to mention that he would be coming round."

"Whatever for?" said Rose.

"It's about doing some sewing," said Toby as he reached the bottom of the stairs.

"You are making absolutely no sense at all Toby, don't worry, I'm sure Andrew will fill me in on what you're trying to explain to me." Rose made her way over to Andrew as he was getting a huge cardboard box out of his car.

"Are you ok Andrew, for what do we owe the pleasure of your company?"

"I take it Toby hasn't informed you?"

"No he hasn't Andrew; he hasn't said a dicky bird. What has he been up to now?"

"Well I hope nothing; however, he said that you have a sewing machine and that you are quite a dab hand at sewing, basically, he has volunteered you to do some sewing for the football team."

"So what's in the box then?"

"Well we were looking for some of the parents to make some football scarves and banners; in the box is all the material. We are looking for about 25 scarves; William McMullan's mum will also be making 25. On top of that, we need a few banners if that's possible.

"Yes of course it is, will Friday be ok?"

"Yes, that will be brilliant Rose."

"Come on in I will make you a brew."

"You have a lovely house, Rose."

"It keeps the rain off my head, once the football at the weekend is over you can come to my house for a meal."

"That would be nice, Rose, thank you."

"Oh hello Mr Mann," said Toby as he came downstairs

"Hi Toby, you can call me Andrew if you feel comfortable with that, obviously at school, it must be Mr Mann or Sir."

"Ok, yes that's fine by me Andrew."

"Thank you for volunteering me to do all of the sewing Toby," said Rose winding him up.

"Sorry, Mum didn't think you would mind."

"Well it looks like I have no choice now, doesn't it?"

"I'm sorry Andrew; I really didn't think mum would mind."

"Well obviously she does, don't worry I will find someone else to do them," said Andrew continuing with the wind-up.

"Toby, can't you see we are winding you up, of course, I don't mind." Andrew and Rose burst out laughing at Toby's expense, and at the same time apologising.

"Thanks a lot, mum, you had me worried then."

"Well, you dish it out enough Toby, so now you need to learn how to take it."

"By the way Rose," said Andrew sipping his tea, "we are telling everyone who is coming to watch the game, to try and wear something along the lines of green, the school; football colours."

"Well I could do with some new clothes, it will give me a good excuse to do some shopping; Holly, fancy doing some girlie shopping later on this week?" shouted Rose from the foot of the stairs.

"I would love to Mum," yelled Holly from her bedroom. It was now time for Andrew to leave and for Rose to get the food on. "I will get started on the sewing tomorrow Andrew, I know you are busy this week so I won't trouble you, just call me whenever you want."

"Ok will do Rose." Rose and Andrew shared an embrace but that was as far as it went with Toby watching from the wings.

It was now Thursday morning and Toby had just gone to school. "Mum," said Holly, "you know that you are not working today?

"Yes, I do know I'm not working today Holly, what is the point you are trying to make?"

"Well if I didn't go to school, then we could go shopping earlier instead of waiting until I come home."

"So what are you asking me, Holly?"

"Well, what I am asking is, why don't you phone the school and tell them I am not well."

"So you want me to lie do you, Holly?"

"No Mum, I would never suggest that," said Holly sarcastically, "I have got a headache, so technically you wouldn't be lying. If you have got a conscience, then just try to look at it that you are bending the truth a bit."

"Oh very well then Holly, don't tell Toby though, I don't want him thinking he can pull the wool over my eyes whenever he wants a day off school."

"Cheers mum, you're a star."

"You can help me finish off these scarves, and then we can go about 11 o'clock." Rose and Holly had a lovely day shopping; they even bought some clothes for Toby. Sat at the dining table admiring their shopping, Rose and Holly lost track of time.

"Is that Toby home already," said Rose, "what time is it?"

"My God, it's 4.15 already mum, just tell Toby you picked me up if he thinks to ask about me being home before him," said Holly.

"Hi Toby, have you had a good day?"

"Yes thanks, mum, you're home early Holly."

"Yes, Mum gave me a lift."

"Oh right," said Toby. "I'm just going to get changed; I'll be back down in a minute."

"Here, take these clothes up with you Toby, I bought them for you today."

"Aww, thanks, mum."

"There's a brand-new tracksuit for you to wear on Saturday, I got you a green one to match your football strip, and I've bought you some new trainers."

"Wow! So cool, can't wait to wear them."

"I do not want you wearing them now, just try them on, and then put them away until Saturday. I'm going out in a few minutes Toby; I need to take the scarves to your school before they lock up. I will do tea when I get back."

"Ok mum, see you later."

CHAPTER 12

MARY THE LEPRECHAUN

Back at Lakeside Secondary School Rose had just arrived. "Hi Andrew," said Rose at the same time giving him a kiss and cuddle. "Got all of the scarves I was volunteered to do."

"Aww, so sorry about that Rose, I'm sure you didn't really mind?"

"No not at all Andrew, I'm just messing. Actually, I enjoyed doing them, here, what do you think of my effort? It took me all week and every minute of my spare time."

"Breathtaking Rose, you're not just a pretty face, I feel heaven-blessed that I met you."

"Well that sort of comment would have been suitable about 20 years ago Andrew, but now, well let's just say, I can visibly see the wrinkles in my face, I will settle for heaven blessed. Anyway, I can't stop, I've got to get to get back and make tea for Toby and Holly; just give me a call when you can. Who do I send the invoice to?

"The invoice," said Andrew.

"Yes, for the labour, it must have taken me about 30 hours at £10 an hour. I make that £300 plus £15 fuel."

"Tell me you're joking Rose," said Andrew with the colour draining from his face.

"Yes, I am joking Andrew, it was just brilliant seeing you squirming."

"I can see where Toby gets it from Rose."

"Anyway, must dash, I will catch you later," said Rose smiling.

"Ok Rose, drive carefully." Friday arrived quicker than expected which meant there was only one more sleep before the big day. Rose was wondering whether or not to try and speak to Tom her husband before the big day. "What do you think Toby?"

"Think about what mum?"

"About talking to your father tonight, I was just wondering whether to try and talk to him tonight."

"Well I need to clear my head and have a good night's sleep Mum, so if you do decide to talk to him, then go for it, you can talk to him from the confines of your bedroom."

"Do you think he will do that?"

"Yes Mum, he has already said he would, why does he have to show himself in my bedroom all the time?"

"Toby Travis; that sounded very disrespectful the way you said that."

"No, I didn't mean it to sound like I was being bad-mannered Mum; I just meant it to sound like that if wants to talk to you or Holly for instance, then he can have a private conversation with you in your own room."

"I know what you meant Toby, just winding you up again, just like you do with me sometimes. I will probably leave it until after the weekend. He is more than likely listening to our conversation now as we speak," said Rose looking up to the heavens. There would be a lot of organising to do tomorrow morning so the Travis household was having a reasonably early night.

Saturday morning arrived quicker than one could blink. Rose was the first to rise out of her warm, cosy bed.

"Toby, Holly come on, time to get up," yelled Rose, I will start making breakfast." It was a mass scramble for the bathroom until finally everyone was sat around the dining table. "Did you speak to Dad last night Mum?"

"Well actually I did, I didn't want to say too much because you need to concentrate on today's football match."

"So he actually came into your room mum, wow, that's cool. So what you are actually saying is, he has managed to find his way from my room to your room without a SatNav, is that correct?"

"Oh no Toby, he has bought a top-of-the-range out of this world navigation system you mad man. What do you think? Of course, he hasn't got a SatNav; sometimes I wonder why I even bother having a conversation with you Toby." Holly was now creased up on the floor listening to Toby and her mum talking like children. "I have had more intellectual conversations with Bob and Brenda's dog than you pair, just cut it out will you," said Holly.

"Well, let's just say that he has become more educated in the way spirits can move around. Your dad actually said that there is a type of school he can attend to learn more about appearing in a more humane way and not just a spiritual figure."

"Right mum, that's it," said Holly, I don't want to hear any more of this comedy sketch, can we just leave it there."

"Fine by me Holly, you mark my word, remember this day and remember this conversation, those words will come back to haunt you one day." With breakfast now over it was time to get ready. Although Holly and Toby were old enough to sort themselves out, it would be Rose who would be taking charge of everything; in other words, if there was something missing when they reached the school, she would be responsible. The Travis family made their way outside to be greeted by cheers from the curtain twitchers Bob and Brenda. "Have a wonderful day Rose, best of luck Toby, we will be thinking about you, see you when you get back."

"Thank you," said Rose and the rest of the family; "see you later."

"Toby, go and give Mary a knock will you, tell her we are about to leave." Just then Mary appeared looking more like an Irish leprechaun: green hat green trousers and a matching blouse. All she needed now was a hairy beard. Toby and his family did their best not to laugh.

"Ok let's get this show on the road," said Rose. Bob and Brenda were still in a state of shock as they couldn't take their eyes off Mary the Leprechaun. After 10 minutes or so they finally arrived at the school. "Wow, look at the coach mum, very smart," said Toby.

"Very posh, bagsie back seat," said Rose.

"Mum where did that come from, you sound like a teenager talking," said Holly.

"I feel like a teenager Holly, got a problem with that?"

"Not at all mum, just try not to embarrass me please." Holly looked over to Toby and whispered in his ear, "I think mum must be in love Toby, hope she isn't going to humiliate us on the coach, if mum sits on the back seat, then I'm sitting near the front." Toby, Holly, Rose and Mary the Leprechaun were now standing with the rest of the crowd, camouflaged by the surrounding trees and bushes. Even though the Headmaster Mr Bamford was tagging along as part of his duty, it was still Mr Symonds's party, in other words, Mr Symonds was totally in charge, along with his assistant Mr Mann. "Ok, can the football team get over here please and the rest of you get on to the coach in an orderly fashion."

"Woo!" said Rose making her children feel uncomfortable once more, "In an orderly fashion, I shall have to consult my children about that one. We left school quite a long time ago Nick, or should I call you Mr Symonds."

"Ok, you are quite correct Mrs Travis, slip of the tongue. Pile on to the coach like a herd of Elephants."

"Now that's better Mr Symonds, I understand what you mean now." Everyone was now in fits of laughter except Toby and Holly who were trying to blend into the surroundings. "Just stand still Toby, they might think we are a tree, just can't believe my mum," said Holly.

"Oh by the way Mr Symonds, please call me Rose, it makes me feel younger."

"Ok Rose, then you can call me Nick."

"How young does our mum want to feel," said Toby to Holly. "At this moment in time, I feel older and certainly more mature than our mum's behaviour."

With all the mums and dads now on the coach and Mary the Leprechaun, the football coaches were explaining what was expected from them when they arrive. "Ok let's have you on the coach," said Mr Symonds. "The journey would take no longer than about 50 minutes all being well, what would be the chance of Rose conducting a sing-a-long and embarrass Toby and Holly once more. A rendition of 'You'll Never Walk Alone' was booming around the coach with their green scarves waving above their heads. Rose was becoming a cult hero with everyone on the coach, I think there were only about two people who were feeling uncomfortable; you guessed it, Toby and Holly. They were thinking about when they arrived back at school on Monday Morning what would be the outcome. The first one would be what an embarrassing mother they have, or.... what a cool wonderful excitable mum you have. "Ok, let's tone it down a little now, save your energy for the match," said Mr Mann. "We are about two minutes away. As soon as we get there just stay in your seats until I find out what is happening." The football ground could now be seen in the distance having everybody staring out of the window. "Wow!!!" said Toby to Liam; "have you ever played at a ground like this?"

"No I haven't, I tell you what though, enjoy the experience Toby unless you or I make it in the big time, this will be our Wembley." The coach pulled up outside the main stand that towered over the coach. You could cut the air with a knife now as the coach pulled up to a stop. Mr Symonds was greeted by one of the supervisors as he stepped off the steps of the coach. "Lakeside Secondary School," said Mr Symonds.

"Glad to meet you," said the steward, "I love your mascot, the best mascot I've seen for a while."

"Sorry," said Mr Symonds, "which mascot are we talking about"

"Your mascot; the green Leprechaun at the back of the coach," Mr Symonds felt like doubling over with laughter but thought better of it; laughing out loud would have caused Mr Symonds a major issue explaining to Mary what he was laughing about. "Oh right yes of course," said Mr Symonds, "we thought so as well, can't come without a mascot."

"Well you can inform your mascot they will be allowed to come onto the field at the beginning of the match with the team, and then also, will be able to cheer on the team from the touchline. What's your mascot's name?"

"Her name, oh yes, her name, she goes by the name of Mary, Mary the Leprechaun. I had to think there for a minute."

"We will give her a mention on the tannoy system at the beginning of the match."

"Oh right, she will love that, thank you so much." The chatting went on for about two minutes before Mr Symonds got back on to the coach to explain what was going to now happen. "First of all, the steward asked me if I have brought a mascot along today, now as you know I never gave bringing a mascot a second thought. Rather than making myself look stupid that I had forgotten about a mascot, I said, and I don't know why, but I said that we had a Leprechaun called Mary."

Fifty heads turned all at the same time towards Mary at the back of the coach. "Are you referring to me?" asked Mary looking shocked.

"Well I kind of got caught off guard Mary, I'm so sorry, I understand if you say no."

"Well, it seems that you have put me in a position where I can't possibly say no."

"I'm so sorry Mary, I understand if you don't want to do it." Within seconds; everyone was calling out her name. "Mary. Mary. Mary. Mary!"

"Ok, Ok I will do it," said Mary chuckling, "Just stop shouting out my name; I don't need reminding what my name is."

"Great Mary," said Mr Symonds. There is a plus side to being the mascot Mary,"

"Oh yeah, and what's that then?"

"You will be allowed on the pitch when the team enters the field, you will also be allowed to run up and down the touchline during the game. Oh yes, and you will be allowed in the changing room when all the lads get changed into their football kit."

"Wow!! Really," said Mary, the look on Toby's face was a picture to behold.

"No, I was only joking about that part of your duties Mary. Ok, now the rest of what was said. On my word all the players and Mary the Leprechaun, I want you to get off the coach and make your way into the stand, the steward will show you where to go. Bring all of your belongings with you. The team stepped off the coach looking very professional trying to emulate the surroundings. "This way Lakeside, said the steward, your dressing room is the one on the left." The lads were amazed at the facilities compared to their school." Wow, look over here William," said Liam, "you could get two football teams into those showers at the same time."

"Yeah, well don't you be getting any ideas, Liam," said Toby; "you won't catch me bending over to pick up the soap." After getting rid of their bags they were told to go and have a feel of the pitch. "This way lads," said Mr Symonds. This was a proud moment for the team as they made their way out of the tunnel and onto the grass surface. The pitch looked gigantic with two seated stands and terraced areas at each end of the pitch. All of the lads had seen a cup final or two before on TV so decided to follow the trend. They made their way around to where the goalposts were for a professional inspection. "Toby, just imagine smashing the ball into the back of these nets," said George Bulldog.

"Would be incredible George," said Toby. Toby put himself into another time zone, while his mates were still chatting away with bewilderment; Toby was standing in front of the goal dreaming of scoring. "You can do it, Toby, you can do it, Toby," said a familiar voice. Toby looked around to see who had said it, only to see that there was no one remotely close to him. While Toby was in his own little world for those few magical minutes, the rest of the team had made their way back to the dressing room without Toby knowing.

"Travis," shouted Mr Symonds, "get over here now." Toby was still feeling stunned by what he had heard. "Dad is that you dad," said Toby looking to the heavens.

"Yes Toby," said his father. "You didn't think I was going to miss the final did you, Toby?"

"Well I'm not sure Dad; my mind was focused on the game if that doesn't sound too rude."

"No, not at all Toby, I completely understand. I have had to put off shopping for the day to be here with you, but apart from that, there is nothing that can't wait until tomorrow."

"Stop joking around Dad, but to be perfectly honest, I'm so glad I have spoken to you, you have taken away any tension I was feeling." Toby made his way over to the sidelines where Mr Symonds was eagerly waiting for him.

"Come on Toby, get a move on lad. Who were you talking to? It looked like you were talking to the heavens. You won't get any help there Toby, these people that believe in Gods and things; I think they have all lost the plot. You make your own luck on planet Earth, that's my philosophy." *If only he knew the truth,* Toby was thinking.

Toby made his way back into the dressing room to rapturous applause.

"Ok lads let's start getting changed, when you've got changed put your tracksuit tops on. Once you are ready, we will get you on the pitch for a warm-up session." Within minutes all the lads were waiting and gathering around trying to keep their minds occupied on the task ahead. "Ok outside, let's go and get warmed up."

Helsby had already made their way to one end of the pitch for their warm-up session, giving Lakeside Secondary their first glimpse of their opposition for the day. "Got some big lads on their team Liam," said Toby.

"Don't worry about them Toby, they are probably saying the same thing about us. Imagine how they must be feeling now looking at George, he would frighten himself if he looked in the mirror."

"Good point well made Liam; I'm glad he's on our team."

"Let's enjoy the experience, Toby, we are not going to lose this match, I won't allow it."

After a ten-minute warm up it was time to make their way back into the changing room for one last time. "Over here Toby," shouted the Lakeside Secondary Leprechaun." Best of luck Toby get out there and knock them dead."

"Thank you Mary, I've no intention of killing anyone, but yes, I will give it my all. If you are looking for something more suited to a horror movie, then talk to George, I'm sure George would be up for it."

There were now only ten minutes to go before kick-off. Mr Symonds and Mr Mann were giving their final pre-match instructions.

"You know what you need to do, it's not a complicated formula," said Mr Symonds. "Get out there and play your own game, don't try and do something that you haven't been trained to do. George, get stuck in, I want you to take control of the midfield area. William, make sure you stay close to George to pick up any loose balls. Chris, I want you to drop back from midfield if William and George are pressing forward; I can't afford to have our defenders exposed. Benjamin McMullan, don't mess around in defence, if you are unsure what to do, then boot the ball out of touch, don't take any chances. Toby and Liam, I don't need to tell you what to do, apart from I want to see that net bulging, you do that, and we win." Just then they got the call from the referee. "Ok Lakeside, let's have you lined up outside in the tunnel."

"Come on lads," shouted Liam. It felt like World War Three was about to start; lined up in tunnel shoulder to shoulder, saw them almost touching the yellow shirts of the Helsby team. The referee made his way to the front of the line, along with his linesmen. Tension was now high as the referee marched them onto the field. There were a good two hundred family and friends shouting and cheering both teams on, Oh and Mary the Leprechaun as they lined up on the pitch. Toby was doing his best to keep his eyes off Mary bouncing up and down on the touchline like a cheerleader. Mr Symonds and Mr Mann had their own seats in the dugout to watch the game from and shout their orders, close to the Helsby dugout.

A few handshakes could be seen from the team coaches as they wished them all the best of British. The Headmasters from both schools shook hands with all the players from both teams. The scene was now set as both teams went to different ends of the pitch. In the centre circle, the referee got the two captains together for the tossing of the coin. "Ok, Lakeside you call; heads or tails."

"Tails," said Liam as the coin was spun into the air.

"Tails it is," said the referee. Which way would you like to kick first?"

"We will stay as we are," said Liam, we will kick towards the south stand." The teams got themselves set up for kick-off. The referee blew his whistle to start the game to the sound of the anticipating crowd. The first five minutes of the game were just a case of getting familiar with the opposition and the speed of the game, tackles were flying in left right and centre with the sound of the referee's whistle working overtime. "Foul, free kick to Lakeside," said the referee in a stern voice. The referee called over the Helsby Captain and warned him about one of his player's behaviour. "The next time I see a tackle like that then you will be a man short, do you understand?"

"Yes," said the Helsby Captain at the same time rallying his troops. The free kick was certainly in a dangerous position about 20 metres out and central to the goal. "Good chance to get an early goal," said Andrew to Nick.

"Would be great wouldn't it, probably too much to ask," replied Nick.

"Come on Lakeside," shouted the crowd. With Helsby now ready with their five-man wall, the referee blew the whistle for the free kick to be taken. It was difficult to know who was going to take the free kick; Liam William and Toby were all standing near the ball. Suddenly Toby and Liam moved to one side leaving William to shoot over the wall and into the top left-hand corner of the net. Nick and Andrew couldn't believe what they had just witnessed, they could be seen punching the air and shouting with delight. "Well done William, great goal," yelled the Green Leprechaun who was jumping up and down on the touchline.

"What a start," said Andrew, to Nick, unbelievable start; 1-0 with five minutes gone." With 25 minutes now gone and some wonderful football being played by Lakeside Secondary School; Andrew and Nick were very concerned that the score was still only 1-0. "Should be more than 1 goal up Nick," said Andrew.

"Yeah you're right," said Nick; "we've had most of the game but just can't seem to get that second goal." With 10 minutes to go until half-time Helsby equalised against the run of play. "Unbelievable," said Nick, "just can't believe what has happened. Come on Lakeside, keep your chin up; let's get another goal before halftime." Two minutes before half time Lakeside were in front again; it could only be Toby Travis. A long ball forward by Benjamin McMullan to his brother William, and then a beautiful shuttled pass to Toby meant Toby only had the Goalkeeper to beat. Toby chipped the ball over the oncoming keeper into the net. "Brilliant Lakeside," shouted Andrew, "no more than you deserve." All the Lakeside followers were now in a jubilant mood, along with Mary the Leprechaun.

The half-time whistle went to great applause and cheers from the Lakeside dugout. "Get yourselves into the dressing room now lads," said Nick, "great first half, well done." Once in the dressing room, it was time for some positive feedback from the two coaches. "Ok lads, we have 45 minutes to go," said Nick. "Normally I would be saying 45 minutes to hold on, however in this case, you are far the better team, unless they have got a Billy Whiz on the sub's bench, then the game is yours to lose. Just carry on playing the same way; if I need to change anything then I will let you know. Have you got anything you would like to add Andrew?"

"Yes, just try and keep your eyes on the ball and not Mary the Leprechaun, she's doing a wonderful job on the touchline so just let her get on with it."

"Thank you, Andrew," said Nick. Just then the referee could be heard calling the teams to get back onto the field for the second half. Helsby were being far more adventurous now causing Lakeside all sort of problems; "Chris get tighter to your man," shouted Nick. "George, you need to track back more; come on lads, more effort is needed. Andrew and Nick were becoming more animated now, they could see if they don't manage to change the way Lakeside are playing then Helsby could get an equaliser. "Get warmed up James, you can take the place of Chris, he's struggling out there," said Nick. Unfortunately, it was too late, before Nick could get James onto the field, Helsby scored once more; 2-2 was now the score, and still, 20 minutes to go.

Silence could be heard at the south end of the pitch from all the Lakeside supporters, as for Mary the Leprechaun, she was looking for a tree to hide in. Chris was now taken off to be replaced by James; it worked a treat. With James getting tight to his man it was breaking up their play and allowing Lakeside to win the ball back. Nick was now so stressed that he was giving his own personal commentary from the dugout.

"Go on James, that's it, pass it to George, well done great pass, out to the wing George, William is free." William received the ball with an excellent pass from George.

"Go on William take your man on, well done William go on lad." At this point, Nick and Andrew were out of their dugout encroaching on the field of play. They slowly started walking towards the Lakeside end and as William got closer to the goal you could see their pace notably getting faster. There were seven minutes left of the game, Nick and Andrew knew this would be their best opportunity of the half so far.

"Go on William," said Nick under his breath, "Toby's on your left, pass it, William, pass it, brilliant ball William. Andrew, Toby's is on goal." Nick and Andrew were now transfixed; it was as if time had stood still as Toby's unstoppable shot rippled the net. Lakeside had made it 3-2 with minutes to go. It was pandemonium, Nick and Andrew seemed to have invented a new type of dance, they were twisting and Jumping, rolling, and humping, squat thrust bunny hops, somersaults, star hops; Mary the Leprechaun was even joining-in with the celebrations. Everyone needed to calm down now, at least for the next 5 minutes. Nick and Andrew were told to get back into the dugout by the referee; it wasn't actually a warning, it was just in the good nature of the game, the last thing the referee needed now was for the two coaches to have a stand-off.

They were now entering the final two minutes which must have seemed like an eternity for all of the Lakeside followers and team. Andrew and Nick were trying their best to control the game from the dugout, just then; a slip from George allowed the Helsby forwards to charge in on goal.

"Oh no," said Andrew, "Get stuck in, don't let him shoot. A cannon ball-like shot struck the post to the sound of "No!!" from Nick. The ball was pinballing around the six-yard box.

"God that was close, oh no," 'Off the line by William,' could be heard, 'great save Mat, get it out lads,' another shot came thundering in only to be deflected for a corner.

"I can't take any more of this Andrew," said Nick, "I can't look. The Helsby Goalkeeper was ordered forward by his coach for one last attack. "Man to man marking lads, one last effort, you're almost there." It felt like slow motion as the penalty area was looking more like Euston station on a Friday night. It would just be a case of preventing the ball from crossing the goal line.

With Nick still refusing to watch the corner, it was down to Andrew to give his radio-type commentary as he counted the minutes down.

"Here it comes Nick, here it comes, No," shouted Andrew, which got Nick to turn around thinking it was 3-3. The ball was picked up by Toby on the edge of the box. With the speed of a greyhound, Toby raced towards the Helsby goal leaving everyone else in his wake, including the Helsby Goalkeeper. Less than 10 seconds later the ball was resting in the Helsby net. Toby had made it 4-2 and on a personal note, he had scored a hat trick.

With the team now rejoicing on the field the referee decided to blow the whistle for full time. The Lakeside Secondary had done it; they had won the Four Counties Cup for the first time in their history. Man of the match Toby for his hat trick had the team carrying him around the perimeter on their shoulders to his embarrassment; in Toby's eyes, the whole team were heroes. The presentation of the cup took place on the field in front of all the supporters. Toby took one last and final look to the heavens; within seconds he saw an image of his dad etched into the white fluffy clouds with a look of approval.

• • • •

TWO YEARS DOWN THE line and Toby and Toby had left school; his mum was getting married and his girlfriend Mary was planning on them following her. His dad had become a fully-fledged ghost now and could appear anywhere at any time; even at the wedding of Rose and Andrew. As for Holly, well her relationship with Liam had fizzled out, it lasted about a year until they both left school and went their separate ways. Holly was working hard at university to hopefully become a lawyer. Toby, well Toby hung up his father's boots on leaving school and is now taking up Judo. What would be the chance of Toby becoming a Judo champion?

About the Author

AUTHORS NOTE

This is my first fictional book after previously writing a 634-page book on my 10 years service in the British Army, and also a 200-page comedy sketch book about learner drivers.

Toby Travis is a young, impressionable teenager that has been brought up by his mother. Unfortunately, Toby and his older sister Holly lost their father just before Toby was born due to a long-term illness. It has been a struggle at times for their mother, who got herself a job down at the local laundrette to make ends meet.

Toby was football mad and was hoping to make the school football team along with his best friend Liam. Having a pair of football boots that his mum could ill afford would be a good starting point. With Toby's birthday imminent, Toby's mum had an idea, an idea that unknown to her and her family would see their world completely turn upside down.

An early morning paper round has Toby drooling over his next-door neighbour Mary and his hormones were kicking in.

Ingram Content Group UK Ltd.
Milton Keynes UK
UKHW010957110723
424927UK00001B/60